THE GLOBAL EARTH/MARS INITIATIVE

The Global Earth/ Mars Initiative

A CONCISE HISTORY OF
THE FIRST THIRTY
YEARS OF THE
GREATEST PROJECT
HUMANITY HAS EVER
ATTEMPTED

James Brown

Guapo Press

This book is dedicated to my family, who listened to me talk (and talk, and talk) about this book with stoicism, encouragement, and, sometimes, even interest. You all helped me to complete what I started. Thank you!

Contents

INFRASTRUCTURE MEGA-PROJECT FUND (IMPF)   117

CLIMATE CHANGE   143

GENERAL HISTORY   175

SPACE EXPLORATION AND COLONIZATION   201

INTRODUCTION

Author Introduction

In May of 1961, President John F. Kennedy requested of Congress funding and faith, stating, "First, I believe that this nation should commit itself to achieving the goal, before this decade is out, of landing a man on the moon and returning him safely to Earth."

This audacious goal led to the United States Moon Project of the 1960s. Striving to meet this challenge pushed us to excel in the theoretical and applied sciences and in engineering. In the summer of 1969, we succeeded in "landing a man on the moon and returning him safely to the earth" and creating a universal confidence and momentum I believe still resonates within the global community.

I was twelve years old when this historical event occurred, and I still remember sitting in front of an old black-and-white television watching it unfold — as did most of the world. I think we were all enthralled to witness an accomplishment that so captured the imagination, that was so beyond what most of us had ever dreamed possible. I know it made a lasting impression on me.

Fast forward to 1991:

The first time I heard the idea of terraforming and colonizing the planet Mars was in a May 1991 *Life* magazine article. Intrigued, I researched the topic and came across several scientific papers by NASA scientists and others describing the theoretical basis for terraforming Mars. I was amazed to think we actually had a shot at doing this.

For the next few years, I talked about this incredible concept to anyone who would listen to me. I must say, there were many heated debates — usually surrounding the need to first fix everything here on Earth before moving on to other planets (I held the opposing view).

Then, during the Christmas season in 2000, I remember thinking hard about global inequalities and the need for more educational opportunities worldwide (spurred, I'm sure, by some new article I had recently read). Something clicked, and I started to see how another bold initiative — akin to the Moon Project of the 1960s but focusing on Mars instead of the moon and involving all nations of the world instead of just the United States — might be just what humanity needed.

I saw how a global initiative to colonize and terraform Mars had many of the ingredients I felt were needed to move humanity in an enduring positive direction. The goal of terraforming and colonizing Mars was certainly as imaginative and bold as the Moon Project — indeed, even more so. Likewise, the initiative would demand a sustained research and development effort that would dwarf anything ever attempted.

However, I also agreed with those arguing we needed to work to fix many of the systems we have abused here on Earth — especially the increased pollution of our planet's air and water systems and the resultant alarming global warming trend. I saw how working on this project would complement the goals widely accepted in the scientific community as necessary to stop or at least partially reverse global warming. I saw that both initiatives would strive for the most efficient use of the world's short- and long-term resources and thus accelerate the reduction of pollution levels. I decided to add this Earth-bound component to my lofty Mars-based initiative, calling the two-pronged project the Global Earth/Mars Initiative (GEMI).

I believe this sustained global effort could, over time, involve tens of millions of people from 200 or more nations of the world. Just as in the 1960s, the scientific demands of this dual initiative would strengthen both the quality and depth of higher education. I also felt that as this initiative gained momentum, the technological advances realized would begin to have broad commercial applications, entering the mainstream of daily life. Logically, ownership of these technologies would be shared in some equitable way among participating nations. Likewise, revenue generated would be shared as well. For most countries of the world, this potentially substantial income could make a big difference in the quality of life for their citizens as other existing revenue streams faded.

For a long time, I simply talked about these ideas. And talked and talked. I finally realized talking was not getting my ideas out there, so I decided to write a fictional account of what might transpire during the first few decades of this initiative through the eyes of a fictional author named William Bookmaker. I chose to write this fictional history as a series of concise essays describing the first thirty years of the project. I felt this format would allow me to identify and summarize the seminal events, movements, developments, and characters in sufficient detail to bring this fictitious history to life for the reader.

I hope you enjoy it.

— Jim Brown

Foreword

Dr. Hana Duarte GEMI CEO, 2025 – 2053

I'm currently sitting in my ISH [Individual Space Habitat], attached to a massive rotating space colony, tens of millions of miles from Earth, researching a book I'm writing about emerging space cultures. I'm just entering my third year as a crew member/researcher on one of the Hubbard Mining Corporation's[1] twin spaceships, HT2. We're mostly replacing crews who have been in space for extended periods, delivering consumables and special material needs – we're a delivery service. We've been to three colonies so far. When we're visiting a colony, I'm free to collect data, do interviews, observe colony societal dynamics – the research for my book. I must confess, I'm beginning to feel like a modern-day Charles Darwin! We're presently at the Pinnacle Colony[2], a mining concern on the edge of Jupiter's L4 trojan asteroid swarm. We'll be heading to the larger Hubbard Colony Complex in a week or so.

I retired in 2053, after 28 years as CEO of GEMI [Global Earth/Mars Initiative], which was about ten months after William Book-maker began this book project. Six months post-retirement, and after a nice vacation with my family in Paraguay, I was off on my Hubbard Spaceship adventure. I have been working remotely with William since then – mostly clarifying first-person accounts of events, fact-checking, things like that – and now he asked me to write the foreword to his book. I am honored.

I met William in 2052, when he was enrolled in one of my cultural classes at the University of Birmingham GEMI satellite office complex. When he first approached me with the book project proposal, he may have been a little overzealous. He described the GEMI treatise he envisioned as one that would take "two or three volumes to complete." I understood why he wanted my assistance – after all, I had been the CEO of GEMI since its inception – but I had no interest in helping to create yet another lengthy, academic GEMI history. I really didn't want another scholarly tome. So, I was pleased when William accepted the conditions under which I would help with the book: write just one volume of bite-sized segments highlighting the creation and development of GEMI, interspersed with relevant contemporary world history. I believed this format, if done correctly, would be of interest to a wide audience. Willliam delivered!

I wasn't too surprised, however. After he approached me about the project, I did some research of my own on William. I found he was a respected postgraduate student with strong writing skills (one of his undergraduate degrees was in journalism). His interest was contemporary history, and his book proposal was part of his doctoral thesis exploring what natural building blocks must evolve in the short term to realize major societal changes in the long term. Very interesting material for a cultural anthropologist. I felt comfortable that the project was in good hands with William Bookmaker.

And, I must say, I enjoyed taking short walks down memory lane. Once, William asked me if any particular moment stood out above the others during my time at GEMI. I had so many memorable times with the organization, but the most impactful for me was when Edward Fisher relinquished control of GEMI, legally handing the keys to the kingdom to Dr. Jacob Baptista [GEMI's Chief Science Officer] and me. I was floored! Really, who would hand over control of an organization worth over $3 trillion? And this was in 2025, when $3 trillion was an insanely large amount. But forget the money. Fisher showed an inherent trust in the process. For him to completely let go like that was incredible – I mean, this was his baby! It had a profound positive impact on me. I took my job more seriously after that. We were now the stewards of this project, we had a world stage, and we had deadlines to meet.

Working with William also had me reflecting on my long working relationship with Dr. Baptista. Fisher was wise in his choice of Dr. Baptista to guide GEMI science. I have fond memories of working with this scientist superstar. His broad, deep grasp of both basic and applied science, his innate engineering skills, and his vision of how to build the core foundation of our space ecosystem were wonderous to witness firsthand through the years. He understood our mission and goals better than anyone, and he expertly leveraged GEMI resources to attain them. GEMI will continue to thrive under new leadership, but we all lost the use of a great mind (and I an occasional horse-riding partner) when Dr. Baptista retired in 2050.

One last thought: Maybe it's the anthropologist in me, but as I was reading the final draft of William's book, I was struck by humanity's general adaptability and altruism, grudgingly, maybe, but still impressive over such a brief period. We came together as a global community – as a global tribe – and have virtually cleaned up Earth and built a solid space ecosystem. It's impressive that nine billion people (who often don't like each other) accomplished all this within a short thirty years. The authors of the Fisher Report [aka the State of the World Report] were correct in this: humanity would respond to a challenge.

William Bookmaker took my "bite-sized segments" to heart and utilized a short essay format to craft a clear, contemporary history of GEMI and relevant world events. He described GEMI's and humanity's biggest challenges, progress, and triumphs eloquently, leaving us (or at least me) enthused for the future. William, through your book, I was reminded how lucky I was to have been involved in GEMI from the beginning. Thank you.

Hana   Duarte   Pinnacle   Mining   Colony,   February   2057

[1]Hubbard Mining Corporation is one of the oldest deep-space colonies. There are more than thirty Hubbard mining colonies, ranging from the staging colony in cislunar space, to the sprawling mining colony in the Jupiter-Sun L4 trojan asteroid swarm region, where more than 1,200 individuals have lived and worked in space continuously for ten-plus years (Hubbard Mining Corporation literature, 2054).

[2]Pinnacle Mining Colony (PMC) is a small space mining colony owned by the Pinnacle Mining Corporation. PMC has been on location at the edge of the Jupiter L4 trojan asteroid swarm since April of 2051, searching for water and organics within targeted asteroids in the swarm. PMC normally houses approximately 2,300 employees and visitors. In addition to its primary mining concern, PMC hosts various scientific and other commercial activities (Pinnacle Mining Corporation literature, 2055).

Preface

Three years ago, while a graduate student studying cultural history in the United States at the University of Alabama at Birmingham, I had the privilege of taking one of Dr. Hana Duarte's cultural anthropology classes at a nearby Global Earth/Mars Initiative (GEMI) satellite facility. I discovered Dr. Duarte would be lecturing for two semesters at GEMI Birmingham (known as GEMI/B) and that she would be using the GEMI Martian subculture as the model for the lecture series. As most of us know, Dr. Duarte is a celebrity in her own right — probably one of the most influential individuals in the world. She led GEMI for twenty-eight years, from its inception in 2025 until her retirement in 2053. Her austere, disciplined life was one of the critical factors in the development of the Martian experience and culture. In many ways, she was the original — the first Martian. This was too rich an opportunity to pass up.

It was a great experience. We explored and discussed the seminal moments and events leading up to the eventual maturation of the Martian subculture. We also examined the dynamics of the "quiet" revolution that paved the way for substantial regions of the world to embrace the Martian philosophy. Dr. Duarte's lectures — especially those that included anecdotal stories about other key people involved in the project — gave fresh, fascinating insights into this period of history. Her recollections of initial meetings with Edward Fisher, and later with Dr. Jacob Baptista, were comical yet insightful accounts that revealed the human side of those we now consider icons.

I'm only 39 years old, so GEMI has always been in my life. For many of us around the globe, it's difficult to imagine the world without GEMI — it's part of the fabric of our lives. Currently, there is one core GEMI-funded research center and roughly eighty satellite facilities in the United States alone. The GEMI Birmingham satellite location is an extension of the Harrison, New Jersey, USA, GEMI Center (one of the original hundred centers worldwide built in the late 2020s). In addition to these hundred centers, another six centers have been opened — all in space. There are also more than 15,000 satellite facilities spread throughout the world. Each year, approximately 200,000 young people (up to a 1,000 from each of 182 countries) enroll in one of GEMI's research facilities to begin their five-year internships before returning home. They are trained in a key theoretical or applied science, industry, or craft, by the world's best minds and facilities. Among the interns, teachers, researchers, and workers of all disciplines, there are over two million people working within GEMI at any given time. Millions have taken this journey through GEMI over the last three decades.

Add to this the financial impact of GEMI. Using straightforward calculations and total transparency, GEMI devised a methodology to share the revenue generated from the thousands of GEMI-owned patents licensed and services used worldwide since the inception of GEMI in 2025. In 2055, the International Monetary Fund (IMF) estimated the dividends from this yearly revenue stream now account for at least 20% of the total revenue for almost half (more than eighty) of the nations participating in GEMI. The IMF also predicted that sometime in the early 2060s, GEMI's gross yearly revenue will exceed China's GDP. Pretty amazing.

Listening to Dr. Duarte's lectures crystallized for me that the ubiquity of GEMI was not always the case. Truly, the last three decades have borne witness to some of the most profound GEMI-influenced global changes in history. I decided to write a book documenting this incredible period in recent history and how GEMI evolved within it.

Towards the end of the second semester of the series, I approached Dr. Duarte with my idea and asked her if she might be willing to spend time on the project. To my surprise, she agreed — but with conditions. I had been considering a full-blown history of GEMI, a grandiose project I estimated would take three or four years to complete and culminate in maybe two or three volumes of a thousand pages or more each. This was not, however, a format with which Dr. Duarte would be willing to assist. She reminded me there were already thousands of existing publications detailing various aspects of GEMI, including a few she had written herself. She did not believe my proposal would add to this body of knowledge in any meaningful way. Rather, Dr. Duarte suggested I focus on a more concise accounting, "…describing the key people and their personalities, the global challenges of this era, and important macro events within and surrounding GEMI. In sufficient detail, this would make for a clear, high-level historical overview of GEMI's first three decades."

Needless to say, I capitulated. The resulting history was written using Dr. Duarte's general template and with her frequent input. This work is neither the scholarly magnum opus I initially contemplated nor a Dr. Hana Duarte biography (although I now want to write one). I believe I have written a history with enough depth and originality to make it worthwhile to the academic community, while revealing some of the flavor of what it was like to live during the time of GEMI's infancy. I hope you find *The Global Earth/Mars Initiative* both informative and inspiring. Surely, in the first thirty years of GEMI's existence, humanity rose up, purposefully shook off thousands of years of cultural ossification, and began building a new era from the ground up — both here on Earth and beyond.

Dr. Duarte, thank you so much for helping me with this project.

Enjoy!

—William Bookmaker

February 2057

Summary

THE GLOBAL EARTH/MARS INITIATIVE

"Historically, most humans are destined to live hand-to-mouth, generation after generation. They depend, in large part, on the measured assistance of those nations fortunate enough to have been created in regions of our small world where environmental conditions favor a more robust and enduring existence. We can end this now."

— Edward Fisher, Global Earth/Mars Initiative (GEMI) founder, in opening remarks during a speech introducing the GEMI project at the World Economic Forum (WEF) Davos Summit, Davos, Switzerland, January 2025

Deeply troubled by chronic, crippling regional economic crises, the increasingly violent social and political upheavals spreading throughout the world, and the general decline of Earth's ecosystems, Edward Fisher, the world's richest man, decided to act. First, he funded an independent *State of the World Report*, quickly renamed the *Fisher Report* by the media. Crafted by hundreds of world-renowned scientists, engineers, and scholars, the 800-page *Fisher Report* presented a grim summary of the world's major social, economic, environmental, and political systems. The authors made dire predictions concerning the consequences of allowing these systems to continue status quo. They then outlined a visionary remedial action plan for the world's leaders.

The authors called for the realization of three bold, interrelated goals. First, the gradual improvement of the human condition across the world population — derived from an enduring change in the distribution of knowledge and wealth among nations. Second, a dramatic restorative effort across the world's major environmental systems, culminating in reducing human-generated emissions of carbon dioxide (CO_2) to "net zero" by the year 2050. Third, the creation of a long-term, audacious, imaginative, near-impossible goal to spark humanity to new creative heights. Using published NASA theoretical work as their guide, they proposed terraforming and colonizing the planet Mars.

They then detailed an inspired road map to achieve these lofty objectives. The first step was the creation of an international organization, manned primarily by researchers and teachers and aided by interns from member nations. These interns would cycle through the organization every five years before returning, educated and trained, to their country of origin. Led by scientists, engineers, and farmers, the researchers would intensely examine and retool everything humans use or consume on Earth — food, energy, clothing, water, transportation, communications — nothing would be exempt. The goal would always be to conserve more and dramatically reduce the use of resources while maintaining functionality. As GEMI-owned technological advances were realized and entered the mainstream of daily life, ownership and revenue generated would be shared equitably among participating nations.

The time-sensitive goals surrounding CO_2 emissions would be met by utilizing the newly created Infrastructure Mega-Project Fund (IMPF). Independent from GEMI, this fund would invest in and manage large infrastructure projects to move hundreds of the world's largest cities towards sustainable, carbon-neutral footprints. The *Fisher Report* authors argued this work would positively impact nearly 50% of the world's population and pave the way for infrastructure best practices across the remainder of the world's population centers.

Finally, citing the United States Moon Project of the 1960s, the *Fisher Report* recommended an audacious goal, akin to the Moon Project but focusing instead on Mars, and involving all the world's nations rather than solely the United States. The long-term goals (adopted from previously published NASA theoretical work) were to colonize and terraform Mars. The authors argued that as humanity strived to meet these goals, we would be pushed to excel in the theoretical and applied sciences and engineering. Also, as we created incremental goals and completed them, we would build sustained confidence and momentum in what we believe our global community can achieve. This project would also be managed within the GEMI core organization.

Agreeing with most of the recommendations in the report, Fisher then began to develop a strategy to ensure the successful implementation of the initiative. He and an eclectic consortium of nations, businesses, and private donors raised $3.4 trillion in startup capital to launch and sustain the core GEMI organization. In addition, Fisher raised $13.6 trillion in investment capital to fund the IMPF, specifically designated to meet the project's time-sensitive CO_2 emission reduction goals. The Global Earth/Mars Initiative and the Infrastructure Mega-Project Fund were born.

Once established, GEMI began its mission in earnest. Within decades, GEMI grew into an immense organization larger than most international business conglomerates. GEMI-based research and development led to a stunning array of scientific, technical, and environmental advances across all industries, both here on Earth and in space. These advances slowly transformed the massive, albeit benign, GEMI into an economic and technological superpower. Likewise, IMPF leveraged private sector capital and expertise to transform the core infrastructures of the world's largest cities while adding trillions of dollars in investment returns to its institutional and individual investors.

The Global Earth/Mars Initiative, written by William Bookmaker in 2057, chronicles the first thirty years of the greatest project humanity has ever envisioned and attempted to execute. The project launched a grand effort involving nearly 200 nations and spearheaded a global movement that forever changed the dynamics among world nations.

Character Highlights

There would eventually be millions of individuals involved in GEMI. Heroes and villains, of course, but mostly quietly passionate workers dedicated to the project's ambitious goals. Most understood, if only intuitively, how the project's incremental successes and contributions were critical to the healthy advancement of humanity. However, early in the project, three larger-than-life individuals pressed their agendas and personalities into the then raw fabric of the project's tapestry. Indeed, it is sometimes difficult to see beyond them to the others who also contributed to the project's success. Looking back through a historian's lens, one can see how the project cohered and flourished across the decades because of the unique contributions of Edward Fisher, Dr. Hana Duarte, and Dr. Jacob Baptista.

Edward Fisher was a driven, eclectic businessman, utterly confident in his abilities. He was famous for methodically collecting the facts related to a decision he had to make — then, after analyzing the findings, acting quickly and decisively. The *State of the World Report* is an excellent example of Fisher's *modus operandi*. He needed unbiased data, so he commissioned the voluminous authoritative report. Once he absorbed the findings, having agreed with most of the recommendations, he acted. Fisher transferred $240 billion of his wealth to the project, and master salesman that he was, convinced other individuals, corporations, university systems, and governments to contribute, eventually raising $3.4 trillion to fund the GEMI project.

After convincing Drs. Duarte and Baptista to accept leadership roles in GEMI, he stepped aside, relinquishing control of the project. Fisher then founded the Infrastructure Mega-Project Fund (IMPF), the largest capitalized corporation in the world. He spent the remainder of his professional life leading IMPF, rebuilding the infrastructure systems of the world's major urban centers, and bringing them in line with the time-sensitive CO_2 emission reduction mandates related to global warming.

From a distance, Dr. Hana Duarte looks like a paradox. She is an accomplished scholar and teacher with hundreds of published scientific papers. She has also authored numerous books on topics ranging from cultural anthropology to functional fitness. She was the respected leader of GEMI from its inception until her retirement in 2053. As such, she built and guided an organization with over two million employees and interns, a yearly operating budget of over $1.7 trillion, and a restricted fund of over $6.7 trillion (2053). However, Dr. Duarte is also known for her competitiveness. She was a world-ranked amateur MMA fighter into her mid-thirties and, within her age bracket, has finished at or near the top in international functional fitness competitions for the last three decades. Still, with all her accolades, throughout her tenure as CEO of GEMI, she continued to participate fully in the randomly rotated maintenance duties of whichever center she happened to be visiting. She cleaned toilets, washed dishes, and labored alongside others in building renovations — whatever was under her name on the center's daily duty roster. Her unpretentious demeanor and innate leadership abilities afforded her the respect of millions of "Martians" through her leadership of GEMI and continues into her post-retirement.

For nearly thirty years, Dr. Jacob Baptista led the largest, most ambitious, and most diverse scientific research and development effort in history. He is the recipient of two Nobel prizes and has been equally successful in theoretical and applied sciences. He is widely considered one of the greatest minds of the twenty-first century. Born in Angola, Africa, in 1982, he suffered the loss of both his parents in the Angolan

Civil War in 1984. A local Christian ministry rescued him, and he was later adopted by an American couple from Raton, New Mexico. They owned a small horse ranch outside of town, and he became enamored with horses, beginning a lifelong passion that he returned to in his retirement in 2050. Urban legend told of him bringing three of his horses to the first GEMI center in Harrison, New Jersey, where they roamed the ground floor of the vast abandoned factory he commandeered for his headquarters.

Dr. Baptista was also famous for constructing large models to mimic those of his inventions and concepts he felt needed concrete, tangible examples. Dr. Duarte once described her amazement the first time she witnessed his horses grazing under massive models of his space elevator and Individual Space Habitats (ISHs) hanging fifty feet from the rafters of his factory office. Usually described as shy, even passive, he was also infamous for aggressively defending his scientific positions, even to the point of physically challenging his detractors. While Baptista contributed to and oversaw tens of thousands of technological advances across the science spectrum, when he retired, he immediately retreated to his family's ranch in Raton, eschewing science and refusing most interviews and engagements.

Biography: Edward Fisher

Edward Fisher
Born: January 2, 1970, Chicago, Illinois
Died: March 21, 2037

An only child, Edward Fisher was the son of affluent, busy Chicago lawyers. He attended private schools through high school, and although he enrolled at MIT on a full scholarship, he dropped out during his junior year to work full-time on various business ventures. Pictures of Fisher as a young adult show a tall, thin man with the big-boned, raw look of a mid-western farm boy (which he was not). Former teachers and fellow students invariably described him as focused and driven, sure of himself and his ability to make the best decisions, while always humble and capable of laughing at himself.

Fisher was a generalist entrepreneur par excellence, and while he never specialized in any one field, he was considered an expert in many industries. His eclectic business acumen, his intuitive sense of risk balancing, and his intense drive drove him to the pinnacle of success. He was labeled the wealthiest individual in the world for a total of twenty-six years between 2001 and 2037.

Fisher founded the Global Earth/Mars Initiative (GEMI) in 2025. At that time, he transferred $240 billion of his wealth to GEMI to help fund the $3.4 trillion GEMI war chest. Within months, he handed over complete control to Dr. Jacob Baptista (whom he named Chief Science Officer) and Dr. Hana Duarte (Chief Executive Officer). Together, they would lead GEMI for twenty-eight years. When asked why he relinquished control of GEMI, Fisher replied, "The report recommended it, and I agreed. The current world leadership — of which I'm a card-carrying member — is not moving towards sustainable solutions to most of our biggest global challenges. I was careful in my selection of GEMI leadership. Now I must walk away and let them do their job, their way." Fisher continued his fundraising efforts for GEMI until 2028, when the organization became fully funded.

Also, in 2025, Fisher founded the socially responsible Infrastructure Mega-Project Fund (IMPF). The fund's narrow investment mandate was to develop and execute large, complex urban infrastructure projects to help meet the time-sensitive international goals concerning CO_2 emission reductions — while making an acceptable return for its investors. The IMPF would grow to become the world's largest private company, with assets of approximately $76 trillion under management the year before its dissolution in 2047. Fisher devoted most of his energies to fulfilling the IMPF mission until his death in 2037 during a terrorist aerial bombing attack on the Kismayo Airport in Somalia. He was survived by his wife of thirty-seven years, Lily Thomas-Fisher. They did not have any children.

An often-cited description of Fisher from a 2016 *Forbes* magazine interview sums up how many of his colleagues perceived him during his long reign as one of the most influential business and philanthropic leaders in modern times:

"Edward Fisher still has the look of youth about him. He has always been brilliant, and early in his business career, he was infamous for his arrogantly reckless attacks on markets, throwing caution to the wind over and over in an attempt to own his target markets outright. The last few years have resulted in a mellowing of sorts. The arrogance is still there but is tempered by a more sophisticated execution of his plans.

"One curious effect of Fisher's youthful success is that he seems caught in a time warp. Like a young rock star whose success necessitates an isolated lifestyle, his mannerisms and slang are reminiscent of the late 1980s, from which he emerged from his youth a successful entrepreneur. Some have misinterpreted this as naïveté, and he has disarmed more than a few competitors, costing them dearly in the marketplace for not taking him seriously. For all his seemingly casual demeanor, Fisher is one of the most skilled and tenacious business sharks the world has ever seen. He never lets go of his targeted business prey until he either has devoured them completely or has eaten his fill and discarded the remains."

Fisher was posthumously awarded the Nobel Peace Prize in 2039 for his humanitarian work related to founding GEMI.

Biography: Jacob Baptista

Jacob Baptista

Born: June 17, 1982, Humpata, Angola

When Jacob Batista was two years old, both of his parents were killed in the Angola civil war. By age three, he was adopted by an American couple who owned a small horse ranch outside Raton, New Mexico. He was a child prodigy in mathematics, and his parents and teachers recognized his gift. They arranged weekly visits to the Los Alamos National Laboratory, a six-hour round-trip drive, for tutoring sessions with volunteer scientists in various theoretical and applied disciplines comprising the lab's scientific community. In a 2015 *Time* magazine interview, he noted how this exposure to theoretical and applied sciences "…more than any other period in my life, shaped my core interests and professional passions. Certainly, I became enamored with the idea of applying theoretical concepts to practical applications — I still am. And it was so cool driving up the mesa to Los Alamos — it's like a scientific fortress at the top of a damn mountain. It fueled many a fantasy for a fourteen-year-old kid."

Dr. Baptista received his undergraduate degree in mathematics at the University of New Mexico in Albuquerque and then attended UCLA, where he was awarded PhDs in physics and chemistry. When asked why he chose UCLA for his graduate studies, Baptista candidly replied, "UCLA was not my first choice, but they had world-class graduate programs and research in what I needed. I'm a lazy guy. I didn't want to be running around the world, catching a degree here and there.

Also, I was still doing rodeos, and I could get to a few good ones from LA. It's as simple as that."

After receiving his degrees, Dr. Baptista accepted a visiting professor position at Princeton University. There, he constructed an important body of work focused on the development of synthetic proteins and enzymes that can spontaneously mutate into antibodies with the potential to combat a broad spectrum of pandemic-class diseases. A few years later, Dr. Baptista also began crafting the model and equations that would eventually evolve into the theory now widely considered the capstone for unifying particle physics. In 2014, he received a Nobel Prize in physics for this work.

Twenty years later, in 2034, he received a second Nobel Prize in economics for his modeling of the multiplier effect. His model was (and still is) considered the best for high-yield regional financial gains resulting from large infusions of capital into a local economy through public mega-projects. In a congratulatory statement, Nuria De León, then managing director of the International Monetary Fund (IMF), stated that "because of Dr. Baptista's model, hundreds of billions of additional dollars have flowed into regions of the world most in need of this infusion."

After Dr. Baptista successfully led the development of the *State of the World Report,* Edward Fisher offered him the position of Chief Science Officer of GEMI, which he accepted in the fall of 2024. Citing the recommendations of the report, he famously — and heatedly — negotiated with Fisher over who would control GEMI policies once the project began. Fisher finally ceded to him, giving Baptista and the (then to be determined) CEO, carte blanche authority within GEMI. Dr. Baptista resigned from his position with GEMI in 2050 with the simple explanation, "The year 2050 has a nice ring to it." He moved back to his family's ranch and immediately stepped out of the GEMI spotlight, refusing to engage in any scientific activities. In a *Raton Times* interview in the spring of 2051, Dr. Baptista said, "I did my job, and we selected a great new CSO for GEMI in Zofia Jankowski. I have my horses and my ranch. I plan to enjoy them."

Biography: Hana Duarte

Hana Duarte

Born: March 5, 1988, Hernandarias, Paraguay

Hana Duarte's family owned a small soybean and cattle farm southwest of Hernandarias, Paraguay. During Hana's childhood, her father was a maintenance worker at the Itaipu Dam while her mother worked the farm, often with Hana at her side. However, by the time she was a teenager, Hana's natural academic and athletic talents began to take hold. As she explained:

"The construction of the Itaipu Dam brought a lot of money into our region. Because of the economic prosperity the construction and maintenance of the dam brought to the region, a few of us local kids were given scholarships to attend schools and universities in the United States and other countries. I was naturally good at sports and an A student, so I was one of them. I graduated from high school at 16 and ended up at UC Davis for both my undergraduate and graduate studies. Davis was a hub for various sports, and I fell in love with triathlons, CrossFit, and MMA. I still train daily. I taught for a few years at UCLA and then was offered a professorship at Vassar. I stayed at Vassar until Mr. Fisher showed up one day. The rest is history."

Dr. Duarte attended the University of California at Davis with a full scholarship, where she earned PhDs in mathematics and cultural anthropology. She stayed on at UC Davis as an adjunct professor of mathematics and anthropology for another two years. She then accepted a tenure-track professorship in cultural anthropology at Vassar College and held this position from 2020-2024.

Fellow students and colleagues described Dr. Duarte as outgoing with a good sense of humor. However, most also noted she was competitive both academically and athletically, and she was no-nonsense when on task.

In 2027, Dr. Duarte won the coveted *Time* magazine Person of the Year award. Jill St. James, one of the authors of the *Time* article announcing the award, describes meeting her for the first time:

"A few of us were lounging on the Passaic River dock on the GEMI campus in an industrial complex in Harrison, New Jersey, waiting for Dr. Duarte to arrive for her interview. One of us pointed towards the bridge just north of the campus, and Dr. Duarte was sprinting across. We watched as she turned onto the road leading to the campus entrance, slowing to a walk as she entered the complex. She walked to a garden hose attached to one of the buildings and rinsed the sweat from her hair and face. She shook her head like an animal, looked up, waved, and headed towards us as she wrapped her hair loosely.

"As she approached, she explained she had been training for an upcoming mountain race. She was covered in dust, her body thin — almost emaciated — but with the look of someone accustomed to hardship and not caring where her next meal came from. Her skin was darkened by the long hours of training in the sun, and her face, arms, and legs exposed sinewy muscle. Hana's hair was the color of India ink with rusty streaks throughout, bunched casually at the top and still dripping water. Her black eyes were always locked on one of us during the interview, piercing and never wavering, and in perfect juxtaposition with the gleaming white of her teeth. She seemed to be alternately snarling and smiling. I felt I was in the presence of an intelligent but wild animal reluctantly choosing to graze — or maybe stalk — among domestic stock."

Edward Fisher offered Dr. Duarte the position of Chief Executive Officer of GEMI in December 2024. She had had no interest in the position and declined his first two offers. Legend has it that Dr. Jacob

Baptista (who had already accepted the Chief Science Officer position with GEMI) came to Vassar and convinced her to take the job. Dr. Duarte retired as CEO of GEMI in 2053, after nearly thirty years. Following a short vacation with her family in Paraguay, she headed to space to research a book she was writing about emerging space cultures.

Partners: Baptista and Duarte

Drs. Hana Duarte and Jacob Baptista had much in common. Both were accomplished horseback riders and raised on ranches. Both were athletes, albeit in different sports. Dr. Duarte was a competitive MMA fighter, triathlete, and world-class CrossFit competitor, while Dr. Baptista was a regionally successful rodeo bronco and bull rider with numerous award buckles to show for it. As well, he competed nationally in Olympic weightlifting competitions until a wrist injury in 2035 forced him to retire.

In addition, they were both respected scientists. Dr. Baptista, considered one of the greatest scientific minds ever, is most famous for his contributions to the Unifying Theory of Physics. However, he also developed a fast-acting family of antigens capable of reacting with a broad spectrum of pandemic-class viruses. As well, his modeling of the use of the economic multiplier effect in large capital projects has realized, over the last three decades, tens of trillions of dollars in local income in the regions where GEMI centers were developed, and IMPF projects were executed.

While not a world-famous Nobel Laureate, Dr. Duarte is still a respected scientist in multiple disciplines, with a lifelong focus on cultural anthropology. She coined the term "ecumenical culture," which formed the basis for her building the sustainable culture and community within GEMI.

They also shared the innate qualities of commitment, discipline, and focus — traits that did not escape Edward Fisher as he percipiently chose the leaders of GEMI. Once the Baptista/Duarte team committed to GEMI, there was no stopping them for the next three decades. Each had a natural purpose within the project, and they embraced these roles. Dr. Baptista relentlessly built the scientific powerhouse necessary to move GEMI towards the goal of terraforming and colonizing the planet Mars. Likewise, and just as doggedly, Dr. Duarte built the community and culture needed to attract millions of individuals to the effort — across almost all known ethnicities, political groups, religions, and countries of the world — both during her tenure as CEO and beyond.

Unlike Fisher, who had a successful long-term marriage, Drs. Baptista and Duarte neither married nor had children during their tenure at GEMI. During a joint interview in 2040, when asked about their enduring single status, Dr. Baptista looked at Dr. Duarte, shrugged, and laughed, "We married the project!"

Author's note: *Dr. Jacob Baptista did eventually marry. In 2052, at the age of 70, he and Lucy McBride, a local retired schoolteacher, were married on Dr. Baptista's Raton, MN ranch.*

The State of the World Report

2024

The *State of the World Report* was funded entirely by Edward Fisher at a price tag of $1.9 billion. The report took eighteen months to complete, with over 300 world-renowned scientists and scholars enlisted in the effort. Fisher commissioned the report to provide him with enough unbiased data to help him make the business decisions necessary to stabilize the world and move it forward along a healthier path. Specifically, the scope of the comprehensive study was to create a detailed baseline of the current state of each of the major world systems, predict what changes might transpire within each system in the near- to mid-future, and, finally, make recommendations on how to make lasting improvements within and across these systems.

The 800-page *State of the World Report* was published in the fall of 2024 and distributed to world leaders at the spring 2025 Davos Summit. Quickly dubbed the *Fisher Report* by the media, the document presented a grim summary of the world's major social, economic, environmental, and political systems. The authors made dire predictions concerning the consequences of allowing these systems to continue status quo. They then detailed a visionary remedial action plan.

In an interview with *The Economist* in 2031, Fisher reminisced about deciding to commission the *State of the World Report*. "We had just wrapped up the yearly Davos Summit — it was 2022, I think — and

I remember being really frustrated. The world was going to shit, and we wasted another year on a dog-and-pony show — always the same. On top of that, we couldn't get reliable data for anything, at least not unbiased data. A few of my colleagues lamented about the need for an authoritative world report, which got me thinking, and I decided to create it. I thought about pulling in other funders but figured it was best to do it myself. Then I could cut through the bull and get it done right.

"So, Jacob [Dr. Jacob Baptista, Nobel Laureate] was a good friend. We were on a few university boards together — we both even owned neighboring ranches in New Mexico. Anyway, Jacob is like the smartest person in the world, the obvious choice to lead the effort, so I decided to ask him to take the role. I called him, explained the project, and asked if he wanted the job. He asked what the budget was. I told him whatever it cost. He said, 'Hell, yes!' It turns out he was still in Europe (he had attended Davos as well), so the next day he flew to London, where I was staying, and we began to make plans."

Dr. Baptista, a small cohort of colleagues, and Fisher identified forty-five categories across the world's major social, economic, environmental, and political systems to be analyzed for the report. For each category, Fisher and Baptista sought out the best minds — undisputed experts in each discipline — to lead the research and analysis. As busy as most of these women and men were, working on an exotic project with an almost unlimited budget was very attractive, and most offers were readily accepted.

All teams had until May 2024 to complete their research and data collection. Then, in early June, Fisher hosted a ten-day summit on the Austin campus of the University of Texas. At Fisher's direction, all researchers attended the summit in its entirety, and along with Fisher and Dr. Baptista, all slept in university dorm rooms and ate meals in campus cafeterias. He wanted everyone focused — no distractions for the duration of the summit.

The final draft was completed by the end of the summit and was published in December 2024. All participating researchers received a copy of the report. This was the same report that, in January 2025, Fisher distributed to world leaders at the annual Davos Summit.

Three bold, overarching, interrelated goals were distilled from the voluminous findings:

1. Gradually improve the human condition across the world population. The authors stated that without sustainable and equitable wealth and intellectual parity across the globe, most other initiatives would fail.

2. Spearhead a dramatic restorative effort across the world's major environmental systems, culminating in reducing human-generated carbon dioxide (CO_2) emissions to net zero by the year 2050. By 2025, most scientists had agreed that global CO_2 emissions must be driven to net zero by 2050 to avoid catastrophic environmental consequences.

3. Create a long-term, audacious, near-impossible goal to push humanity to new creative heights. Adopted from published NASA theoretical work, the report proposed terraforming and colonizing the planet Mars. The authors argued that humans need to explore, need challenges, and eventually need to colonize beyond Earth.

Author's note: *In January 2027, GEMI held its first annual seven-day planning summit and has continued to host this annual summit through the present (2055). Modeled after the original Fisher Summit, the GEMI Summit is hosted at one of the GEMI centers. Participants (primarily GEMI scientists) must commit to attending for the duration of the summit.*

Colonizing and Terraforming Mars

2025

One of the earliest legitimate proponents of terraforming Mars was NASA Senior Scientist Dr. Christopher P. McKay. Dr. McKay received his PhD in astrogeophysics from the University of Colorado and worked at the NASA Ames Research Center in California. He began publishing papers on how to terraform the planet Mars in the mid-1980s. *Life* magazine picked up on his ideas and, in 1991, popularized the idea of terraforming and colonizing Mars with a lengthy article that included a pictorial walk through the process.

McKay's idea was to introduce a massive chemical catalyst on Mars to induce the release of greenhouse gases from various sources on the planet. Through a centuries-long process, this would thicken the atmosphere, increase the ambient surface temperature, and, in turn, stabilize liquid water on the surface of the planet. However, by the early 2020s, subsequent explorations of Mars had supplied researchers with more geophysical data. This data led most scientists (including NASA researchers) to conclude there probably was not enough accessible CO_2, using existing technologies, to produce the greenhouse warming effects necessary to bring about the terraforming of Mars.

But Dr. Jacob Baptista, GEMI Chief Science Officer, disagreed with these conclusions. From the inception of the GEMI project, he funded research of the Mars terraforming and colonization efforts. In 2037, the

GEMI advisory board criticized the continued focus on GEMI-funded research in technologies related to the terraforming of Mars, stating the intellectual and financial resources used for this research was excessive and irresponsible. Dr. Baptista responded, "As stated in the *Fisher Report* thirteen years ago, the goals of colonizing and terraforming Mars are audacious in scope. Yes, it will be damn near impossible to realize. Just like, in 1961, President Kennedy set a goal of 'landing a man on the Moon and getting him back to Earth safely,' was a crazy, impossible, audacious goal. And yet, by God, they did it.

"GEMI is going to continue to aggressively work to meet the stated goals of colonizing and terraforming Mars. We're making solid progress — hell, we already have colonies on both the Moon and Mars. But don't hold your breath waiting for substantive progress in terraforming the planet. As you all know, the timeline for this is hundreds of years. This might take a wee bit longer. ..."

Author's note: *While the first manned mission to Mars was in 2031, GEMI, to this day, continues aggressive R&D in its quest to terraform Mars. Of special note: Dr. Baptista observed in an interview in 2049, "Over the last three decades, this body of work has led to a deep understanding of the process of forming greenhouse gases (GHG) here on Earth. This research has been instrumental in the dramatic reduction in GHG and the reversal of the climate-warming trends the world had experienced up until 2052 (the first year since the mid-1950s that the average world temperature decreased)."*

THE GLOBAL EARTH/MARS INITIATIVE (GEMI)

In the world of the late 2050s, GEMI is essentially ubiquitous. However, this was not the case in the early years of the project. It is important for the reader to understand how GEMI and its two leaders were perceived when the project was founded and, at times, only grudgingly accepted by the world. As you will soon see, Drs. Hana Duarte and Jacob Baptista wasted no time in working through the goals dictated by GEMI's lofty mission.

GEMI in a Nutshell

GEMI in a Nutshell

2025

Edward Fisher founded the Global Earth/Mars Initiative (GEMI) in 2025 to act on the recommendations of the *State of the World Report.* Fisher funded the report and, initially, GEMI, himself and convinced the most famous living scientist, Dr. Jacob Baptista, to lead the scientific effort as the Chief Science Officer. He introduced the initiative to world leaders at the spring 2025 Davos Summit and, over several years, raised $3.4 trillion to support GEMI operations. Fisher also hired Dr. Hana Duarte, a virtually unknown cultural anthropologist, to manage the GEMI organization as Chief Executive Officer. Surprisingly, Fisher then handed over the control of GEMI to Drs. Baptista and Duarte and removed himself from any leadership role within GEMI.

The report called for the development of a hundred research and development centers worldwide. While efforts were made to place centers in third-world countries, all were placed primarily based on functional needs. All centers were assigned specific research areas in energy, clothing, shelter, communications, infrastructure (waste, water, energy, and transportation), and space-related technologies, based on GEMI's goals to examine and retool everything humans use or consume on Earth — and what we will need to take the next steps in space[1]. To satisfy the universal need for sustenance, all centers were also responsible for researching and refining local food and water security practices.

As of 2055, there are 106 centers worldwide, including centers located at the South Pole; an ocean ship-based center (with a small flotilla of satellite ships); centers in each of the poorest eighty-two countries of the world (and several in more affluent countries); a center within the GEMI Space Colony 1 (GSC1); and centers on the Moon and on Mars. GEMI employs approximately 2.15 million participants spread through its network of centers. Roughly one million are interns who live and work at the centers. An estimated 15,000 satellite offices account for another 750,000 employees. The remaining 400,000 are regular employees — mostly research scientists and professors, along with a small cadre of administrators at each center.

Full membership in GEMI is limited to sovereign countries. Each participating country must pay a one-time sliding-scale fee based on its average GDP from the last three-year period. They then receive one million shares of non-negotiable stock in GEMI. In keeping with GEMI's core goal of redistributing wealth across all countries, as revenue is realized from GEMI-developed and commercialized technologies, dividends are distributed annually to member countries based on this stock ownership[2]. For the fiscal year ending in 2054, the International Monetary Fund (IMF) reported that the dividend payout to each member country reached $22 billion. For the countries at the bottom 10% of the economic food chain, this windfall accounted for an astonishing 40% of their yearly GDP.

Another goal of GEMI was a global redistribution of knowledge. To accomplish this, each member country is invited to send up to 1,000 of their brightest young people per year to GEMI centers for five-year technical internships at no cost[3]. During this time, participants study theoretical and applied sciences related to their chosen technical specialties, and they spend their last one to two years working within their selected fields. At the end of their five-year tours, they return to their country of origin as trained professionals[4].

GEMI's advisory board seats approximately 500 members. Every member country is invited to elect a board member, as are major private donors, corporations, and university systems participating in GEMI.

However, the board is strictly used to exchange ideas and communicate broad plans and timelines to the world. The board meets annually at a different host GEMI center during the annual GEMI Conference[5].

---

[1]GEMI has historically partnered with space-facing companies to reach its space R&D goals.

[2]In a unilateral act of generosity, in 2027, each G20 member country agreed to contribute its one million shares back into the stock pool for redistribution to the remaining member nations. Within months, an additional twenty-eight nations in the next economic tier agreed to do the same. Years later, it was discovered that Edward Fisher had lobbied the leaders of all these countries for this concession, attempting (successfully) to maximize the annual dividends for the poorer countries.

[3]GEMI does not charge any tuition for the five-year internship. However, room and board are paid for by the intern's country, based on a sliding scale. The cost of room and board is kept to a minimum through tight budgeting and transparent itemized billing. Dr. Duarte once commented, "Almost all our interns through the years enthusiastically help keep expenses down at the centers. The itemized approach gives them immediate feedback. It works very well for us and saves the member countries a lot."

[4]On occasion, interns will request to stay for one or more years beyond the five-year agreement. With permission/arrangements from their home country, they are normally allowed to do so.

[5]The GEMI Conference once coexisted with the long-standing Davos Conference, where Edward Fisher introduced GEMI to world leadership. The GEMI Conference eventually replaced Davos entirely. The last Davos Conference was held in March 2031.

Edward Fisher Moves Forward with Project

Edward Fisher Moves Forward with Project

2024

Edward Fisher was born and raised in Chicago in an upper-middle-class family. He developed a strong social conscience, and, throughout his life, he exhibited empathy for those living in poverty. While his parents were corporate lawyers, they were also heavily involved in local work with the poor. In various interviews, Fisher confirmed their dedication to eradicating poverty, citing both his mother and father as significant influences in molding his drive to build a better, more equitable world.

In January 2022, Fisher, as he had for nearly two decades, attended the annual Davos Conference. However, his frustration with the poor quality of the data, the general apathy of attendees, and his peers' inability to take what he considered to be real action was the last straw. For Fisher, it came down to empathy for the world's poor, coupled with his innate drive to solve large, complex problems. He perceived the vast challenges of the world as discrete problems and was convinced that with focus, discipline, and enough capital, they could be solved — and his sense of responsibility, his proven business abilities, and his brilliant, analytical mind gave him the confidence and energy to move forward in doing just that. He decided to commission an authoritative *State of the World Report* to assess what was needed to get the job done.

The report cost close to $2 billion and took eighteen months to complete. After reading it and reviewing the findings with his friend and the report's lead scientist, Dr. Jacob Baptista, and others, he decided the project must move forward.

In his memoirs, Dr. Baptista described witnessing Fisher's decision to move forward with the GEMI project: "For Edward, the report and the data were vital. I mean, Edward was a well-informed layman regarding the state of the world's major systems, but he needed more unbiased data and advice before he could decide on his course of action. So, when he approached me about leading the effort to create the report, essentially giving me a blank check to do so, I figured, why not? It was an intriguing project, and I was happy to accommodate Edward's desire to get the straight facts.

"Fast forward a year and a half later. In August of 2024, when the report was complete, Edward met with me and a handful of other scientists for a last discussion of the findings. He had attended our final ten-day retreat in Texas in June, but he wanted to pick our brains one last time. For most of the day, he reviewed the report with us, especially the recommendations. Edward was beside himself and kept getting more agitated as we worked through the report. Anyway, towards the end of the meeting, Edward flatly told us he was moving ahead with the project. I remember we were all taken aback. For most of us in the room, this was just an academic exercise. It's one thing for someone worth $350 billion to spend a couple of billion to scratch an itch, but he was committing to raise and spend trillions to make this project a reality. A few of us suggested he take more time to consider his options, but his decision was made — we were going to do this."

Baptista Asked to Lead the GEMI Scientific Effort

Edward Fisher and Dr. Jacob Baptista met for the first time at the annual Davos Conference in 2013 and quickly became friends. Fisher, the richest man in the world, had always been a student of science. Dr. Baptista was the most recognized scientist of modern times, having already been awarded one of the two Nobel prizes he would eventually win. As co-panelists at the conference, they discussed the efficient use of the multiplier effect in mega-projects, a topic on which both were experts.

From early 2023 until the completion of the *State of the World Report* (aka the *Fisher Report*) in June 2024, Dr. Baptista led the effort to develop the report. This had been a significant time commitment for him, so when Fisher reached out to ask him to lead the project recommended in the report, he declined, citing his many obligations and research interests. He did not have the time to run an organization as large as the report demanded.

However, Fisher knew Dr. Baptista's mix of expertise in the pure and applied sciences was perfectly aligned with the planning, research, and development across the scientific disciplines identified within the project. He needed Dr. Baptista to make the project happen — so he offered to split the responsibilities. Dr. Baptista would assume the role of Chief Science Officer, with total control over the research and development efforts of the project, and they would find someone else to take on the role of CEO for the project — essentially an administrator handling the day-to-day activities. But Dr. Baptista again declined. Fisher later explained Dr. Baptista's rationale: "Jacob understood better than I did what we needed in a leader. He knew hiring a conventional administrator would almost certainly erode the project over time. He told me as much when he turned down the second offer."

When Dr. Baptista refused the second offer, he described what he thought would be needed in an individual who could lead the project while keeping it fresh and challenging for the long term. Dr. Baptista said in his 2052 autobiography, "I told Edward we needed to find a young, smart, brash candidate with no business experience. Also, whomever we selected had to be given complete control over how the organization was developed and run. He [Fisher] had to remove himself from the equation. We had to break out of the mold — totally break from how the world's 'leaders' had been screwing things up for so long. I kind of had a 'wild thing' envisioned in my mind. With Hana Duarte, we succeeded in spades. A damn Amazon woman with two PhDs!"

While Fisher initially resisted giving up control of GEMI, he eventually agreed. In turn, Dr. Baptista accepted the position of Chief Science Officer, assuming the role in November 2024. Together, they began the search for the out-of-box leader Dr. Baptista envisioned. They finally found the best candidate in Dr. Hana Duarte, a Cultural Anthropology and Mathematics professor at Vassar College in Poughkeepsie, New York. She eventually accepted the offer and began her term as CEO of the GEMI project in early spring 2025.

Fisher Recruits Dr. Hana Duarte to Lead Project

2024

The authors of the *State of the World Report*, aka the *Fisher Report*, explicitly warned not to use traditional (meaning, unsuccessful) remediation techniques or personnel when executing the GEMI plan. With pressure from Dr. Baptista, Fisher acknowledged they had to heed this warning and embrace the unpredictable and unconventional in putting together the GEMI structure and leadership. From that point, he developed the GEMI strategy to ensure the project would, to the extent possible, always work outside the box, allowing it to be as unpredictable as necessary and not controlled by conventional leadership.

Dr. Baptista, and eventually Fisher, understood that one of the project's greatest dangers was the long-term lethargy inherent in almost all large institutions, corporations, and governments — especially those well-financed. They had witnessed this firsthand in many corporate and academic institutions. If they were to allow this weakness to infect the project, it would fail.

Fisher recalled, "With prodding from Jacob, I finally understood and accepted that I was also a part of the establishment — that I was not immune to old-fashioned thinking. This is why we needed strong, unique leaders such as Hana Duarte and Jacob Baptista. Duarte because she is brilliant, charismatic, and stubborn — and naive. Baptista because he — I don't know — how can I describe him? His mind is so different from any other. He has, as we all know, no filters. But the way he processes data! His mind is almost certainly one of the greatest the world has ever seen. And his humility and total disregard for all social norms somehow allow him insights and solutions that most of us would not see. Still, I must admit, while I was certain Baptista and Duarte were the best choices to lead GEMI, I was very uncomfortable not knowing what directions in which they might take the project. Ironically, this unease convinced me I was making the right choice in handing over control of the project to these two wonderfully unique and unpredictable individuals."

Once Dr. Baptista accepted the offer to lead the science effort in the project, he and Fisher quickly narrowed the CEO search to one candidate, Dr. Hana Duarte, a professor at Vassar College. Fisher and Dr. Baptista made their famous first visit with Dr. Duarte shortly after noon on November 12, 2024, on the Vassar main campus. Below is a somewhat comical excerpt from an interview with Edward Fisher and Dr. Baptista in the June 2027 issue of *Forbes* magazine, describing the encounter.

Dr. Baptista: "Oh, yes, I remember our first encounter with Dr. Duarte well."

Fisher: "Now Doc, you're not going to rehash that lame version again, are you?"

Dr. Baptista: "Edward, every word of it is true. You know it."

Fisher: "Right, right. Did we get her to sign on in the end?"

Dr. Baptista: "Yes, we did. Now, would you please allow me to continue?"

At an expressive wave of Fisher's hand, Dr. Baptista continued.

Dr. Baptista: "Initially, Dr. Duarte had no interest in the CEO position with GEMI. Her reasons were clear — she was a tenure-track professor at Vassar, actively teaching in her disciplines (mathematics and anthropology), and she felt comfortable socially within the Vassar campus environment."

Fisher: "Tell them about the fight! Wait, let me. So, we stop by one of her offices, and some student tells us to check the gym — that if she wasn't teaching, she was probably there. So, we drive over to the Vassar gymnasium and wander around until we hear what sounded like punching and kicking. We walked into a large room towards the back of the building, and there she is, fighting some big guy in a makeshift ring in the middle of the room. We start to get closer, and we're stopped by, I don't know, the coach maybe. He asks why we're there, so we tell him we need to talk to Dr. Duarte, and he tells us to wait by the entrance. So, we're like standing there with our mouths open as she kicks his ass. I mean, she literally spun around and cold-cocked this guy. Drove him to his knees!"

Dr. Baptista, chuckling: "Yes, what Edward said. She was amazing."

Fisher: "Right? Damn near knocked his head off! Anyway, she helps him up, then she's talking with the coach, who points to us. Next thing, she's coming our way — breathing heavy, no shoes, a tank top, sweating. Drying off with a small towel...."

Dr. Baptista: "Edward..."

Fisher, nodding: "Okay, okay. Anyway, she comes up to us and asks what's up. We introduce ourselves and offer her the job. She refuses. End of story."

Dr. Baptista: "Not quite the end. We agree to meet with her later the same day in one of her offices to discuss the position."

Fisher: "And — she refused again."

Dr. Baptista: "Yes, she did, but you couldn't blame her. As I said, she was content at Vassar. It really is a beautiful, quaint campus. Still, Edward's correct. But we did eventually convince her to accept the position."

Fisher: "With your help."

Dr. Baptista: "Yes, with my help. Once she understood she and I would be running the show — that was the kicker."

Fisher: "That and the horses...."

Dr. Baptista, nodding and laughing: "Yes. I owned a few horses and planned on bringing them with me to whichever Center campus I lived on. She liked that."

Author's note: Dr. Duarte finally accepted the position of CEO of GEMI on January 5, 2025. A very generous donation to Vassar College from Edward Fisher ensured her multiple-year teaching contract was terminated without penalty.

Davos and the Project Announcement

2025

> *"Historically, the majority of the world's population has been destined to live hand-to-mouth, generation after generation. ... This state of affairs must end."*
> — *Excerpt from Edward Fisher's 2025 Davos Conference speech*

For six decades, the World Economic Forum (WEF)'s annual five-day Davos Conference brought together 3,000 world leaders in business, politics, academics, and religion to discuss the state of the world. While no longer active, the yearly Davos Conference was famous for gathering the world's power elite. Each year's agenda included a mix of approximately 400 sessions, during which attendees would describe and dissect projects, plans, and challenges associated with altruistic global themes. Still, there were always dramas and deals to work through behind the scenes among those powerful or rich enough to be invited to the conference.

Each conference began with an opening awards ceremony, with scheduled talks by four or five of the most prominent thought leaders of the day; each speaker would pontificate on one of the critical inter-related topics identified for the year. This opening act set the tone for the gathering, with seminar tracks and roundtable discussions spinning off the main themes for the remainder of the conference. Fisher had used his influence to secure an invitation as one of these influential speakers. Further, he made sure his talk would be the last, ensuring he would have the audience's full attention and set the topic for the remainder of the evening's table talk.

While Davos resort staff published the *State of the World Report* to the private WEF website for the nearly 3,000 participants scattered throughout the conference venue, Fisher's aides, likewise, handed out tablet versions of the report to the hundreds of dignitaries attending the ceremony. After his introduction, Fisher walked to the podium and turned toward the audience, smiling widely and announcing, "Ladies and gentlemen, thank you for inviting me to give this last talk of the evening. I promise I will keep it short."

True to his word, Fisher completed his talk in less than eight minutes. While he felt this was the perfect forum from which to launch the GEMI initiative, he did not want his audience to misconstrue his announcement. His goals were to explain GEMI to the world's leaders, distribute the report so they could read it at their leisure, and, most importantly, put world leaders on notice: He had decided to act.

Many historians have analyzed the voluminous minutes from the subsequent sessions and recorded discussions from the 2025 Davos conference. The consensus was that most of the leaders in attendance did not yet fully understand and appreciate the significance of GEMI. Indeed, most of the sessions dedicated to GEMI were conceptual in tone. Regardless, Fisher later claimed in an interview that he probably received verbal commitments of over $500 billion from conference attendees who pledged to contribute to the project.

Transcript of Fisher Speech at Davos

2025

"Ladies and gentlemen, thank you for inviting me to give this last talk of the evening. I promise I will keep it short.

"Historically, the majority of the world's population has been destined to live hand-to-mouth, generation after generation. They depend, in large part, on the measured assistance of those nations fortunate enough to have been created or unified in regions of our small world where environmental conditions favor a more robust and enduring existence. In the last few years, this situation — coupled with the long-term greed and repressive behavior of local regimes — has led to desperate and dramatic political and social upheavals, and I believe there will be more to come. This state of affairs must end.

"Three years ago, I decided to fund a comprehensive state-of-the-world report based on careful research and input from hundreds of the world's best minds. My associates are distributing the report to you now.

[As Fisher spoke, aides wheeled out carts and distributed tablets containing the *State of the World Report* to everyone in the room.]

"The gist of the findings: All of our major world systems are broken, and there are no promising remedial plans or projects on the horizon to deal with these fundamental faults. The report concludes with a dire warning to us all — one we cannot afford to ignore. If we do not act quickly to fix these systems, and as the consequences of global warming manifest, we will experience more and more desperate revolutions from a growing number of nations and regions. Anarchy will become the norm instead of the exception. The report recommends strongly that we act decisively and boldly to improve the human condition across all nations and regions; work aggressively to reduce human-generated emissions of CO_2 to net zero by 2050; and revitalize the human spirit through the creation of a universally shared, audacious project that is far-reaching in its magnitude.

"I believe these findings are irrefutable, and I have decided to do something about it. I have formed a neutral organization that has three interrelated missions.

"First, this organization will work to improve the human condition by redistributing knowledge and wealth among nations.

"Second, through intensive research and development, we will rethink and retool virtually everything humans consume, use, and interact with during our day-to-day lives. Food, fuel, transportation, shelter, communications, clothing, space exploration — everything — will be up for review and revision, always with the aggressive goal of reducing energy and resources, moving us towards net-zero CO_2 emissions by 2050.

"The third mission of the organization is to colonize, and eventually terraform, the planet Mars. It's an audacious goal that, in our lifetimes, will also firmly establish our ability to safely explore, live and work in space.

"All sovereign nations are welcome to participate in this project voluntarily. Each year, we will invite a thousand individuals from each participating nation to work and study, as research interns, at one of a hundred world-class research and development facilities strategically placed, for the most part, in impoverished regions of the world. Each intern will commit to five years of study and work within the project, followed by returning to their country of origin, hopefully, to make good use of the knowledge and experience they obtained.

"Each participating nation will be issued stock in this organization. We believe, over time, this organization will begin to accumulate more and more relevant technologies and patents. As these technologies become more pervasive, their use globally, and the corresponding revenue generated, will become a substantial revenue stream for the member nations. We believe this earned revenue, coupled with the profound knowledge shift gained by the cycling of people through the organization's research facilities, will, over time, create a more sustainable economic parity across nations.

"Some nations may decide not to participate in this organization, and of course, this is their choice. However, in my opinion, this would almost certainly, over time, put them at an economic disadvantage. Even the largest industrialized nations would begin to lose economic relevance if 180-plus other nations built and participated in intellectually and economically powerful alternatives to the way we participate in globalization now.

"We are financing this massive project by soliciting wealthy individuals and families, as well as corporations small and large, and by collecting member nation dues. To date, we have collected $960 billion. Within the next twelve months, we will be finalizing the nation membership initiative. By then, the project will have amassed a projected $3.4 trillion in funding commitments. At that point, we will begin to bring the interns from the member nations into the project[1].

"In the meantime, we have assembled the core team of 300 scientists and administrators, including the Chief Science Officer, Dr. Jacob Baptista, and the Chief Executive Officer, Dr. Hana Duarte. This announcement is the official launch of what we are calling the Global Earth/Mars Initiative, or GEMI. We are in business. If you have any questions concerning how to participate, there is a section in the report that explains the process. Thank you very much for the opportunity to use this forum to make this exciting announcement."

---

[1]GEMI actually began hosting a limited number of interns in 2025, at the first center, located in Harrison, New Jersey.

$3.4 Trillion Amassed

2028

Against all odds, Edward Fisher, then the richest man in the world for over twenty years, orchestrated an unprecedented accumulation of liquid wealth. Within three years of founding GEMI, he amassed $3.4 trillion[1] and set the stage for the decades of prodigious accomplishments to come for this unique organization.

Fisher accomplished this feat by organizing what was, essentially, akin to the largest IPO in history. Technically, the offering was not an IPO because individuals could not purchase stock in the project. Still, 80% of GEMI stock was "sold" to the nearly 200 countries that signed on to the project. Each country received one million shares of stock in GEMI, regardless of their investment. Contributing corporations and institutions received the remaining 20% as non-voting stock, with all potential future dividends pooled into what would be distributed evenly to the member countries. However, ownership of this stock gave all participants a seat — and a voice — on the member advisory board Fisher formed.

The average cost of the buy-in for a country was $12 billion. For perhaps a third of the world's countries at the time, this number was more than their GDP; as such, these countries could not afford this steep price. Fisher recognized this deficiency and devised a sliding scale cost model based on each country's GDP in relation to the entire pool of participating countries. However, the result was still that each participating country received the same one million shares of stock.

Initially, many of the wealthiest countries balked at the tiered fee. They argued that since the benefits were identical, the membership fees should be as well. Fisher acknowledged this inequality but refused to change the requirements, stating, "All countries must have skin in this game, but let's be realistic. It's unfair to charge a country with a $20 billion GDP the same as a country with a $20 trillion GDP. We're just not going to do it." Nevertheless, only two countries declined membership. Ironically, both were third-world countries (Togo and Benin).

Fisher understood that as GEMI began to generate substantial revenue from the growing portfolio of new technologies produced within the project, GEMI stock dividends would also grow. For poorer countries, this cash stream would eventually become a substantial portion of their national GDP. Fisher was adamant that this potential cash cow would forever be a national treasure and perennial economic windfall for them. For this reason, he devised a plan to ensure member countries retained their stock ownership.

Fisher severely limited the conditions under which stock could be tendered. No stock could be sold, traded, or transferred for the first forty years of the project (until 2062). At that time, the stock could trade hands; however, the stock immediately became Class B stock (non-voting and essentially worthless).

Approximately two months after the Davos announcement, Fisher hosted a four-day conference to educate representatives of prospective member countries and give them talking points to assist them in selling the project to their home country's leadership and citizens. During the conference, the details of the stock offering were reviewed, as well as the short- and long-term intellectual property and revenue-generating dividend potential for member countries. In addition, the five-year intern program was fully detailed.

Each country had six months to work through its internal political processes and sign the agreement, and an additional three months to finalize its financing arrangement with GEMI. In the end, the 98% buy-in rate was due in part to the well-organized conference, the intrinsic fairness of the legal structure of the project, the attractive short- and long-term financial projections, and an almost universal trust in Fisher.

---

[1]The collection of the $3.4 trillion took several years to complete. However, to Fisher's credit as a shrewd businessman, 97% of the committed funds were realized by 2028.

About the GEMI Centers

The authors of the *State of the World Report* (aka, the *Fisher Report*) recommended establishing a hundred research and development centers worldwide and doing so, where possible, in economically depressed regions. Collectively, these center communities would serve several purposes. They would train hundreds of thousands of interns from almost every country in the world in a wide range of applied sciences; engage in targeted research and development of new technologies and methodologies to address inefficiencies in everything humans use and consume in the world; infuse needed capital into the host regions; and assist humanity in furthering space exploration and colonization.

GEMI Chief Science Officer Dr. Jacob Baptista and his team determined each center's general geographic location based on the environment and resources needed for the scientific work planned for that facility. They utilized local agents to find properties, negotiated long-term leasing commitments (most are 50 years or more), and handed each project off to local GEMI project managers to bring the centers to life. By the end of 2027, ninety-nine of the original centers were at least minimally operational.

Center campuses ranged from renovated industrial complexes (such as the first center in Harrison, New Jersey, in the United States) to newly constructed complexes similar in look and function to a high-tech R&D facility or small research university. Indeed, *Forbes* magazine once described GEMI as a "...very well-endowed university with a decision-making board with only two members —Drs. Hana Duarte and Jacob Baptista." When asked if this was an accurate description of GEMI, Dr. Duarte shrugged and responded, "Well, we are well-funded, and Dr. Baptista and I pretty much run the show. But we're not a higher education system, we don't have degree programs, and we don't do quantitative subject matter testing. The interns are essentially here to learn a trade, albeit a bleeding-edge high-tech trade. ... "

There are similarities between GEMI centers and university systems. However, GEMI centers focus on teaching and training interns to support the research and development for which the center is responsible — in other words, training to fill a particular functional need. While there have been detractors through the years criticizing this limited scope of learning, GEMI's tens of thousands of patents, and widely successful alumni, attest to the wisdom in this methodology. Still, each center offers ad-hoc second language courses, support courses, and ongoing seminars on relevant engineering topics utilizing the largest multimedia repository in the world, covering all sciences. Interns are expected to use these resources to fill any education gaps exposed during their five-year GEMI tenure.

In executing its scientific mission, GEMI centers would develop working business relationships with thousands of companies, non-government organizations (NGOs), and university systems worldwide. However, as a cultural anthropologist, Dr. Duarte understood that each GEMI center also needed to gain the trust of and maximize its positive impact on its host community. "We're here for GEMI's science, of course. But another — and equally important — component of GEMI's mission is the gradual improvement of the human condition," she said. "Each center helps move us closer to this ambitious goal. We typically have dozens of satellite offices and clinics propagate within the local communities surrounding each center, assisting the people with just about everything — mostly for free. And each center's carefully managed economic multiplier adds billions of dollars per year to the local economy."

Certainly, the addition of the centers into mostly chronically economically depressed regions of the world has been a boom for the corresponding local economies. In its *2054 World Economic Outlook* update, the IMF estimated that "nearly one trillion dollars was infused into developing regions last year because of the presence of the GEMI centers."

As of 2055:

- The median cost to build and equip each center was $2.1 billion (in 2025 dollars). However, there were extreme cases at both ends of the spectrum. While the South Pole and Guyana centers each cost less than $100 million to complete, the Space Elevator Center ($18 billion) and the Pleiades Space Colony ($69 billion) were huge expenses, even with GEMI's deep pockets.

- The current annual median cost to maintain each center is $3.3 billion (in 2055 dollars).

- There are currently 106 GEMI centers. There are 102 Earth-bound centers, two space colony-based centers, one on the Moon, and one on Mars.

- Approximately 1,100,000 interns, 300,000 researchers, and 100,000 employees occupy the GEMI centers.

- Approximately 22% of GEMI interns, researchers, and employees live within the physical GEMI centers. The other 78% live in standard local community or special purpose housing[1] financed by GEMI.

- 97% of the food consumed across all centers was certified organic with no negative CO_2 footprint and was either grown within the center proper or purchased locally.

- The average annual GEMI center-generated economic multiplier effect for the local center host region is $8.9 billion (not including annual national dividends from GEMI).

- There are approximately 15,000 GEMI-managed satellite offices worldwide (an average of nearly 50 per center). There are about 400,000 GEMI employees working at these offices.

As the centers developed and thrived, so too did the regions hosting them. GEMI's ongoing operations, its altruistic satellite offices, and the stable influx of capital from thousands of new jobs and businesses in GEMI center locales have helped once economically depressed regions and countries more confidently plan and build their futures. GEMI centers emerged in the 2050s as polestars for their local host communities' financial, environmental, and professional enrichment.

----

[1]By 2032, GEMI owned or leased over 500,000 intern housing units worldwide, far exceeding American Campus Communities, Inc., its nearest competitor, at 140,000 units.

First Center Opens in Harrison, NJ

2025

Edward Fisher purchased the Harrison, New Jersey, USA center for $9.2 million in late November 2024, shortly before making his famous Davos announcement. The complex included six large brick factories totaling approximately one million square feet of space, located on twelve acres along the Passaic River. Fisher began renovations immediately. However, Dr. Hana Duarte requested that all interior finish work be left for the interns to complete. She wanted the interns to have some responsibility and ownership in constructing their living and working spaces. Dr. Duarte also requested that a 30,000-square-foot open space on the ground level of one of the buildings be reserved for sports activities. The property was cleared; the docking on the waterfront was rebuilt; minor construction work was done on each building to ensure structural integrity; and new electrical, plumbing, and heating systems were installed. By the time Dr. Duarte arrived in May 2025, most of the work had been completed — at the cost of $17 million.

The Harrison Center officially opened on June 15, 2025. However, most of the core administrative staff had taken residence during the first two weeks of May, including Dr. Duarte. The only exception was Dr. Jacob Baptista, who had been at the Center since late March. He had commandeered an entire building for his headquarters and even brought three of his ranch horses to the Center, housing them in a large open-bay area on the ground floor of the building he occupied.

Until more centers were operational, GEMI invited the approximately 190 member nations to send just three interns each to this first center location. Most of the influx of interns took place during August. As best as they could, they limited the number of interns arriving each day to no more than forty. For the next two months, Dr. Duarte or one of her assistants would drive to Newark International Airport to pick up interns and bring them to the Center. By the end of September, 558 interns from 186 member countries had begun their five-year internships at the GEMI Harrison Center.

While local contractors were enlisted where needed, the interns were responsible for building out the living and research facilities — everything from hanging windows and doors to installing sheetrock, laying flooring, configuring data cabling, and even constructing a dirt path meandering throughout the property. Dr. Duarte made sure all necessary communal areas were operational. Each building had a large industrial kitchen/eating area, baths, and fully installed heating and cooling systems.

When asked what she remembers from the early days at the Harrison Center, Dr. Duarte was quick to provide a few anecdotes. "We had no clue what we were doing. When we — administrators, teachers, and researchers — began showing up May, we were totally unprepared. It took us until August to get everything settled. I mean, we still had to finish our living quarters and get enough of the research spaces and offices in order so we could all get started on our duties. Jobs, pay, food, social activities — we scrambled all the time. Then, the interns started arriving at the Center early in August. Everything started again with more people, from, like, 190 different countries — almost 600 interns. The languages, cultural differences, food, up to four people sleeping on cots in bare rooms while we worked to get their quarters ready. But we all made it through. The interns were great — they jumped in, helping wherever needed. We got the job done."

The Harrison Center was designated an administrative/logistics hub for GEMI and remained the symbolic core of GEMI throughout Dr. Duarte's term in office as CEO. It was small compared to most of the other centers, but it was close to New York City and nearby Newark International Airport. It was especially convenient for Center-based personnel traveling to/from New York City or using the airport often.

Author's note: GEMI administration carefully applied carbon credits to offset the CO_2 emissions they used by traveling by airplane — credits they were earning by the millions, from GEMI reforestation and other carbon-credit generating programs operating at various centers worldwide. After 2036, with the advent of hydrogen-powered international flights, this, of course, was no longer necessary.

Interns

2027

GEMI invited each member nation to send up to 1,000 interns each year to participate in GEMI's Intern Program[1]. Each intern committed to a five-year stint living, studying, and working at one or more GEMI centers. While their schedule might vary depending on what field they studied and worked in, all interns went through an extensive orientation. Each intern studied theoretical and applied topics within their field for two to four years, followed by one to three years of working within a research project, before returning to their country of origin.

For the success of both the intern and GEMI, it was essential to align each intern with a curriculum and field of study/work best suited to their capabilities coming into the internship. As such, GEMI worked with each nation to screen applicants based on education level, aptitude, and work experience. The country's future human resources needs were also taken into consideration. After the optimal track was determined for the intern, GEMI analyzed availability across its 100 centers and placed the intern at the center with the training/work program that best matched the intern's profile.

Once they arrived at the center, each intern was allotted approximately twenty square meters of private living space. The assigned location for each intern was randomized to facilitate a more comprehensive and personal daily interaction across the multitude of cultures within each center. Each center's cohort of interns would go through a one-month orientation period together. During this time, they would be introduced to the center, the host country, the norms of both, and the larger center community, including their peers, teachers, and the general research/development work environment in which they eventually would be involved.

Most interns willingly followed the norms and regimen of both GEMI and their local center, taking satisfaction in the routine that allowed them to focus on their studies and work. In addition to studying and working within their field, each intern was assigned several hours of center-related work each week. This included grounds work, cooking, cleaning shared spaces, and physical renovations. No one was exempt from these duties, and it was common for center administrators to be working alongside interns cleaning toilets. Even Dr. Duarte was on the duty roster of whichever center she happened to be visiting.

Approximately four years into an internship, GEMI counselors would begin working with each intern and their home country to help place the intern into the optimal position when they completed their five-year stint. Where they landed depended on the field the intern was trained in, their level of expertise, and their desire for further training or to enter the workforce. On occasion, when there was a specific need, GEMI would request the intern be allowed to continue working within GEMI. However, GEMI always served as strictly an advisor; the interns and representatives of their countries of origin determined the post-internship decisions.

Author's note: Cohorts varied in size but averaged fifty interns each, with a new cohort arriving at each center bi-weekly. After the first five years, this amounted to a zero-sum gain in that roughly fifty interns arrived, while fifty returned to their country of origin twice monthly.

---

[1]While GEMI covered the cost of training, room and board costs were the responsibility of the intern's country of origin (or the interns themselves).

An Early Hana Duarte Interview

2026

In late spring 2026, one year after taking up residence in the first GEMI Center in Harrison, New Jersey, Dr. Hana Duarte, as the new CEO of GEMI, agreed to a local media interview. Below is the complete *Star-Ledger* newspaper article, dated Sunday, June 7, 2026.

Born in 1988 on her family's soybean farm outside of Hernandarias, Paraguay, Dr. Hana Duarte grew to excel in scholastics and athletics. She was awarded a full scholarship to UCLA, where she received PhDs in both applied mathematics and cultural anthropology. She taught at her alma mater for a few years before accepting a position teaching cultural anthropology at Vassar College. Fluent in five languages, Dr. Duarte is a world-class functional fitness athlete and an accomplished MMA fighter who still trains daily.

Now, at only 38 years old, she is the CEO of the largest startup in history. Founded by Edward Fisher, the world's wealthiest person, the Global Earth/Mars Initiative (GEMI) has amassed $3.4 trillion in financial commitments from almost 200 nations and thousands of businesses, organizations, and individuals. This unprecedented funding will support a grand plan to distribute wealth and knowledge more equitably across the globe, help reduce CO_2 emissions worldwide, and eventually colonize and terraform the planet Mars.

With a corporate structure somewhat unique to the business world, GEMI has two leaders: Dr. Duarte, who as CEO, will guide the administrative and community development of the hundred centers worldwide, where most of the scientific research and development will occur; and Dr. Jacob Baptista, the CSO, who will lead the science itself. Dr. Baptista is widely considered one of the greatest scientific minds of modern times — he is the recipient of Nobel Prizes in physics and economics and something of an eccentric celebrity — while Dr. Duarte is a relative unknown outside of her immediate academic circle. With about $700 billion in hand and the balance coming incrementally over the next several years, Drs. Duarte and Baptista are already moving quickly to prepare GEMI to work through the organization's ambitious mission.

Dr. Duarte agreed to meet us at the new GEMI Center/Headquarters, a converted factory complex on a twelve-acre industrial parcel along the Passaic River in Harrison. She met us in the compound parking lot, and we walked a hundred yards to one of the six brick factories, alongside of which was a makeshift picnic area overlooking the river. Dr. Duarte offered us water, raw vegetables, and fruit as we sat on mismatched plastic chairs surrounding a large, battered wooden spool table.

Below is a short excerpt of our interview with Dr. Duarte, which can be found in its entirety at www.enewssl.nj.com.

Star-Ledger: Dr. Duarte, thank you for agreeing to this interview. Before we begin, please don't take offense, but it smells like a farm here.

Dr. Duarte (laughing): Yes — it's the horses! Our resident cowboy, Dr. Baptista, brought three of his horses with him from his ranch in New Mexico. Seriously, he's a real cowboy. Owns a horse ranch, rides rodeo broncos — the real deal. He took the building closest to the river for his offices and work. He converted a few of the rooms on the ground floor into stalls and put up a paddock from the back of the building down to the river. His horses graze there all the time. I love that smell. It reminds me of our family farm in Paraguay. We have horses too.

Star-Ledger: Dr. Duarte, from what I understand of the project, GEMI — under your and Dr. Baptista's guidance — will, in the next few years, build approximately one hundred research and development centers in as many countries, spending hundreds of billions of dollars to get these centers ready for the work ahead. These GEMI centers will house an enormous, diverse group of individuals — within the next few years approaching one and a half million scientists, employees, and interns from 200 member countries. Do you feel prepared for this challenge?

Dr. Duarte: Not even close. Until recently, I was an untenured professor of cultural anthropology at a small private college. I have no experience that would prepare me for this. Ironically, Mr. Fisher told me upfront my inexperience was one of the prerequisites for the job! After he explained it to me, I understood why — and I agreed. But, still, it's unnerving to think about the scope of the GEMI mission and our role in it all. I am so grateful for Dr. Baptista's involvement. He might be unconventional, but he's also the best scientist in the world to lead the scientific effort within GEMI. We work closely on projects every day. I value his experience.

Star-Ledger: Surely, Mr. Fisher is also willing to weigh in on the more important GEMI decisions.

Dr. Duarte: Actually, no — and believe me, I tried. Mr. Fisher relinquished control of GEMI when Dr. Baptista and I were appointed to our positions. He refuses to even give his opinion of our decisions. And he's a busy man, what with all the IMPF [Infrastructure Mega-Project Fund] work. We haven't even talked for maybe a month now.

Star-Ledger: There is an unprecedented amount of funding for this project. I recently read $700 billion in cash has been collected already, with another $2.7 trillion committed and projected to flow into the project over the next several years. That's $3.4 trillion — a mind-blowing amount.

Dr. Duarte: It's closer to $800 billion now. And yes, it's an insanely large amount. I still haven't wrapped my head around it. Still, given our goals — the build-out of the centers — and the upkeep of each, the ongoing cost of R&D, the interns, space exploration … yeah, I can understand why the price tag is in the trillions. Still hard to believe, though.

Star-Ledger: Then there is the goal of terraforming and colonizing Mars. This seems nothing short of science fiction. Is this a serious and realistic goal for GEMI?

Dr. Duarte: Well, it's one of our core goals, so we're going after it. Realistic? That's a question for Dr. Baptista. But I can say when I read about terraforming and colonizing Mars in the report, I thought, they sure met the audacious, near-impossible criteria with that one!

Star-Ledger: So, Dr. Duarte, you must be very busy. What is a typical day for you here at the Harrison Center?

Dr. Duarte: Busy? I guess. I start my day early with a run. Then I do chores — help cook breakfast for everyone, washing dishes afterwards, latrine duty — whatever's on the day's chore posting. Then I work on center-related business. I also meet with Dr. Baptista most days to go over R&D portions of each center's buildouts. Then another workout in the late afternoon.

Star-Ledger: Latrine duty?

Dr. Duarte: Yeah, once in a while. We randomly rotate duties.

Star-Ledger: So, you and Dr. Baptista have already selected where each center will be located, and what R&D work will be done where? That seems fast.

Dr. Duarte: Well, Dr. Baptista and dozens of other scientists and engineers who now work at GEMI worked on creating Fisher's *State of the World Report* too. They're the experts. They identified most of the center locations and what they needed for their research back then. That earlier work is helping us a lot.

Star-Ledger: We recently ran an article about your staff helping the local Harrison community by voluntarily cleaning up sections of the immediate area surrounding your center. You work with the local homeless population, too — showers, hygiene, food, shelter. You even converted a smaller building on the property into a homeless shelter, of sorts. How did these initiatives come about, and will you continue the practice?

Dr. Duarte: Well, an intern began cleaning up outside our center perimeter shortly after they arrived. Within days, a bunch of us were out there with them. One thing led to another and, yes, we now have a homeless shelter at the center. I mean, we wanted to engage with the local host community anyway. These were simple ways to begin. And, yes, we'll keep at it.

Star-Ledger: Do you think Mr. Fisher's expectation of you as an unorthodox and unpredictable leader is accurate?

Dr. Duarte: I don't know, and I don't really think about any expectations Mr. Fisher might have beyond our following our mission. I respect Mr. Fisher, of course, but he hired me with his eyes open. It's important for GEMI that we don't second-guess ourselves while we develop what we believe is the best way forward for the organization. I'm sure he expects that of both Dr. Baptista and me.

Star-Ledger: So, next steps for GEMI?

Dr. Duarte: Well, there's a lot to do. We'll be opening another ninety-nine centers within the next couple of years — about four new centers a month. And we'll be growing our numbers as the centers come online. Then we have relationships to build with staff, interns, member countries, each of the center host communities. Again, Dr. Baptista is a big help. He's collaborated on so many scientific projects around the world. He's well-known everywhere, and he's opened many doors for us already.

© Star-Ledger (2026)

__Author's note:__ The effort to assist local communities continued as GEMI opened centers around the world. In the late 2020s through the present (2055), this community service orientation was expanded and formalized to include thousands of satellite offices — all dedicated to helping the local populace.

The GEMI Manifesto

2025

Within months of taking office, Dr. Hana Duarte published a simple eight-point GEMI manifesto that has, for more than thirty years, guided millions of employees and interns and influenced hundreds of millions of people worldwide. At the time, she gave a special thanks to the attendees of the Davos 2020 Summit, citing the Davos 2020 manifesto as her inspiration for the GEMI version. She explained her rationale for using the Davos manifesto as a model for GEMI, "It had most of the elements I felt we needed. I saw no reason to come up with something uniquely GEMI. I just simplified the Davos wording and gave them due credit for the portions I used."

The GEMI Manifesto

1. Involve everyone in the project in reaching our goals.

2. Stay the course; do not deviate from our mission.

3. Treat everyone like you want to be treated.

4. Be an active local community member.

5. Be honest and utilize an unbiased mentor.

6. Be fair with and trust all partners, but demand transparency.

7. Buy locally whenever possible.

8. Work to improve the world's environment.

Scholars have interpreted and dissected the GEMI manifesto along political and religious lines through the years. However, Dr. Duarte rebuffed these speculations, reiterating a statement she gave shortly after publishing the manifesto in 2025: "The manifesto had nothing to do with politics or religion. I laid the framework for a robust

community-based culture, with concentric community involvement —
each center's community, the larger GEMI community, the center's
local host community, and the world community. And I wanted the
manifesto to be equally adoptable not only to every intern and employee of GEMI, but also to the organization itself.

"I tried to engage Jacob [Dr. Jacob Baptista] in helping me with the
manifesto, but he was focused on his science. He did get a little excited
about my including the local multiplier effect — that's number seven
on the list. Always the scientist, he is passionate about the phenomena
and how to maximize it.

"There were lots of questions surrounding numbers five through
eight — mainly how they related to both the individual and the organization. With number five, it was all about transparency and not
drifting. For each individual, it's having someone you can confide in,
someone who knows you and can put you back on course if you stray.
Organizationally, each of our centers will have a small group of local
citizens periodically reviewing metrics associated with the local center
— but not an executive board. We want opinions based on transparent
data, but we may or may not agree, and as long as we're not breaking
any laws, we're not asking for permission.

"For our partners in number six, we're primarily interested in
vendor supply chains. Did they make every effort to remain local? Are
their labor practices ethical? We don't demand they adhere to all of our
organizational precepts, but these are deal-breakers. Number seven is
all about the multiplier effect, which is central to our mission. We
always want to maximize the influx of capital into the local community
and then keep cycling this capital back into the same pool for as long
as possible.

"As for number eight, we're all responsible for the stewardship of
the world's environment. Nowadays, this is baked into most of what
we do. However, back in the 2020s, there was no framework, no real
accountability, at just about any level. Back then, I felt we needed to
clearly state this obvious need."

GEMI's Twenty-point Project Roadmap Criticized for Its Limited Scope

2026

In the summer of 2026, Drs. Baptista and Duarte quietly published a twenty-point high-level project roadmap for GEMI's next twenty-five years. Many world leaders were quick to criticize them for omitting or scaling back on several *Fisher Report* recommendations. They were mainly concerned with what they considered a lack of emphasis on reducing CO_2 emissions. Don Gerrish, Managing Director of the International Monetary Fund (IMF), led the attack, stating: "Of course, we all care about our clothing and holistic health [both roadmap goals]. However, we have larger issues at stake in our world, and we would rather see more emphasis on reducing CO_2 emissions worldwide. Almost our entire membership invested heavily in the Global Earth/Mars Initiative, based on the recommendations of Edward Fisher's *State of the World Report*. We expect an acceptable return on our investment."

While Drs. Baptista and Duarte did not respond to their detractors, Fisher did. He bought full-page advertisements in the *New York Times* and the *Wall Street Journal* and used them to lambaste those criticizing the GEMI roadmap for their short-sighted view of the project and its goals. He cited numerous projects within the GEMI roadmap and their positive effects on CO_2 emissions and global warming.

He then noted that the GEMI mission had not changed, stating, "GEMI will focus on broad research and development across most of what humans use or consume in the world, always striving to reduce our carbon footprint. GEMI will help redistribute wealth and disseminate knowledge across nations, and GEMI will help build the means for humanity to live and work in space."

Ever the salesman, Fisher ended the ad with, "If you simply want to make money investing in a green fund, invest in the IMPF — I will do my best to realize a profit for you. However, if you want to make public statements about GEMI, praise it — for it is doing far more than any other organization to repair our world."

GEMI Twenty-point Project Roadmap

After a full year on the job, we better understand the profound responsibility GEMI has to move specific global agendas forward. We are also more rooted in the realities of coordinating the research and development effort necessary to keep an enterprise as immense and diverse as GEMI on track. In the spirit of transparency, we decided — for ourselves and our member nations — to lay out what we plan to focus on for the next twenty-five years. We think of it as a high-level to-do list.

1. Virtual reality (work/health)
2. Living and working in space
3. Space elevator
4. Space colony development
5. Global warming / CO_2 emission reductions
6. Food and potable water security
7. Renewable energy
8. Clothing
9. Center development
10. Ocean cleanup
11. Transportation (Earth)

12. Transportation (Space)
13. Communications
14. Redistribution of wealth
15. Knowledge dissemination
16. Holistic health
17. Regionalism
18. Housing
19. Reforestation
20. Cultural diversity

We are developing a detailed work plan with a budget and specific short- and long-term goals for each initiative. As we finalize each set of goals, we will publish them. We will also review progress for each at least annually with our membership.

We did not include timelines as there are too many variables involved. However, we are committed to the following two crucial milestones:

- All Earth-bound centers will be operational by the spring of 2028. Most will likely not be completed, but they will be livable, and our interns and researchers will be in residence and able to work.
- The space elevator will be operational by 2038. We consider this a pivotal component to eventually living and working in space. Without an elevator, we are dependent on propulsion-based vehicles. This would severely limit our ability to move the necessary resources from Earth into Space – and continue to pollute our atmosphere. Indeed, we see the space elevator as the world's gateway to space.

Author's note: *GEMI delivered on both promises. All one hundred centers on Earth were at least minimally operational by the winter of 2027. The space* *elevator became operational in 2035 — three years ahead of Dr. Baptista's prediction.*

Centers Take Shape
around the World

2025 – 2055

By the close of 2027, all one hundred original GEMI centers were operational, although it would take several more years to complete the build-outs for most. Physically, each center was unique, usually reflecting the local climate and social and economic environment in which they resided. However, while GEMI made efforts to align each center with its local environs, functionally, each was primarily built to meet the research and development needs of the center's resident scientists. With the basic research facilities, and living quarters in place, Drs. Jacob Baptista and Hana Duarte could fully populate each center with researchers and interns and move projects forward.

The first GEMI center opened in 2025 in Harrison, New Jersey, in the United States. Dubbed HUSc (Harrison United States center), it is the administrative headquarters for GEMI, occupying an twelve-acre compound in an industrial park on the banks of the Passaic River. The center is in a heavily populated metropolitan area and thus has an urban ambiance, enhanced by the 2,000 GEMI employees and interns from nearly 200 countries comingling with the local community. Drs. Baptista and Duarte moved into living quarters there in the spring of 2025. Dr. Baptista lived at HUSc for two years before moving to the Tiras Mountains, Namibia Center (TNc). Dr. Duarte called HUSc home for her entire tenure at GEMI, only moving back to her home country of Paraguay after her retirement in 2053.

Over time, GEMI personnel — aided by like-minded local volunteers — cleared, repaired, cleaned, and painted most of the public spaces within roughly a half-mile radius of HUSc, including the shore of the river and many city blocks. Visible from commuter trains leading in and out of New York City, the compound has become both a tourist attraction and an oasis for the local community flocking to the weekly HUSc farmer's market or just enjoying the paradoxical pristine beauty of this industrial oasis.

Below are descriptions of four representative centers from around the world, each with different (though sometimes complementary) scientific goals, but all with the same overarching GEMI mission.

Tiras Mountains, Namibia Center (TNc) — The largest GEMI center houses more than 37,000 women and men living and working on the sprawling, ranch-like campus. Strategically situated in the Tiras Mountains of Namibia, Africa, the center encompasses 315,000 acres and spans several unique ecosystems. TNc R&D goals include the development of arid plant husbandry techniques to produce nutrient-dense, plant-based desert foods; urban commuting alternatives that utilize advanced virtual reality; and hyper-energy-efficient rural housing options.

The ongoing shift to regionalism and rural living that began to accelerate in the early 2030s created a demand for optimized rural communities. As such, TNc has become known worldwide for its expertise in developing models that optimize the long-term use of all available natural and man-made resources within rural settlement ecosystems. To keep up with steady demand, TNc personnel travel to regions around the world, assisting thousands of communities in learning to live better lives with what is locally available.

South Pole Center (SPc) — On the other end of the spectrum is the smallest Earth-bound GEMI center, which houses sixty-five interns, researchers, and staff. Modeled after the Amundsen–Scott South Pole Station, the movable, modular, elevated center contains approximately 42,000 square feet of living and work quarters and cost $96 million to build. The location of the center was selected because its starkly desolate and hostile climate closely resembles the Mars environment. In fact, the original six Mars astronauts trained at the SPc.

Into the late 2050s, the center still focuses on optimizing the minimal life systems needed for living in harsh off-Earth environments. The SPc also specializes in training simulations for space-bound personnel involved in mining operations on asteroids and other planets.

Ship-based 1 Center (SB1c) — SB1c was GEMI's first ocean-based research ship in a fleet that would eventually number six ships at sea. The SB1c has a permanent crew of thirty-two and an intern/researcher cohort of up to seventy-four. Ongoing research goals include the cleanup of ocean plastics pollution; alternative electricity generation; sustainable ocean-based food sourcing and management; and the development of floating and submerged communities.

All the ships were previously owned and were refitted to facilitate GEMI's research needs. In a speech delivered at the SB1c's inaugural launch, Dr. Baptista acknowledged, "We were inspired by Mr. Røkke's [Kjell Inge Røkke, Chairman of Aker ASA] amazing research yacht, the REV Ocean, and sort of ran with the idea of a flotilla of refurbished research vessels. Our ships are not as large as the REV, but they are very well-equipped utilitarian vessels nonetheless."

Space Colony Center 1 (SCc1) — The SCc1 was the first GEMI space-based center, established when the GEMI near-Earth space colony, the Pleiades, was released from the ISS and maneuvered into its own near-Earth orbit in early 2028. Still operational, the colony currently encompasses fifty-three ISHs attached to nine hubs. It houses 300 full-time interns and staff, plus about fifty workers in short-term transit status. The SCc1 also serves as a way station for the GEMI space elevator, routing supplies from the elevator's near-Earth platform to other colonies within near- and mid-Earth orbits.

As of 2055, there were 106 centers, with five new space-based centers in the planning stages. Four of these will be within space colonies, while one (slated to go live in 2058) will be the first "shuttle spaceship," traveling in four-month loops between Earth and Mars. This next-generation spaceship will shuttle people to and from emerging space-

and Mars-based colonies. It will double as a center and have active R&D goals.

Author's note: *Dr. Baptista famously hand-carved the masthead for the SB1c, using Dr. Duarte as the model.*

Ecumenical Culture: A Cornerstone of GEMI

2048

The authors of the *Fisher Report* described the global decline of local cultural norms and the movement towards cultural homogenization as "insidious and dangerous consequences of both economic globalization and a ubiquitous media presence worldwide." They argued that the continuation of these trends would lead to a systemic weakening of the human race and underscored the scientific axiom that diversity is essential to all life forms and should be nurtured and protected at all costs. The authors cautioned that in pursuing the goals of the Global Earth/Mars Initiative, cultural diversity must be maintained and nourished.

Dr. Hana Duarte, as a trained cultural anthropologist, agreed with their assessment. Since the inception of GEMI, she drove the development of a clear set of norms within the sprawling organization to ensure the project stayed on mission while fostering healthy cultural identities for all participants. Dr. Duarte nurtured the positive aspects of intermingling a large number of cultures together. At the same time, she decided not to focus on culture within day-to-day living at the centers, concentrating instead on living and working together towards common center-based scientific and community goals within a clearly defined set of societal norms.

In an excerpt from an article Dr. Duarte wrote for *Cultural Anthropology Journal* in its spring 2048 publication, she explained her philosophy and strategies regarding the management of so many cultures within GEMI:

"When Edward Fisher described the project to me in 2024, one of my first thoughts was, how can we embrace hundreds of cultures within such a large, geographically diverse group of individuals? In retrospect, while the first few years were bumpy, for the most part, allowing the interns to freely express their cultural norms within our communities has been easier than we anticipated.

"We take the time during the orientation of our interns to educate them in what we're about — the importance of a broad theoretical and applied scientific education; specialized training in a relevant work field; healthy living through physical activity; eating well; taking care of yourself; empathy for others. We've structured a pattern of daily living virtually anyone can step into without compromising their native cultural heritage. We encourage thoughtful interactions with other people.

"In building a foundation for center-based community living, the expression of one's cultural identity is essential. As we build this foundation, we examine how each component potentially impacts an intern's core cultural values and how we can maintain those values. This has been key for us. It's gotten easier over time — I mean, we've had millions of interns cycle through GEMI over the last three decades. Still, for each new intern, it is critical that they go through this process. GEMI has a set of norms we all need to follow. More importantly, when an intern returns home after living and working within GEMI for five years, their cultural identity should be — if anything — stronger."

Author's note: Over the past thirty years, all interns have been asked during orientation to describe cultural characteristics of their home country that they consider important. GEMI has collected and cataloged this large body of anecdotal descriptions of cultural practices and combined them with carefully recorded discrete data pertaining to each intern, including sex, age, and ethnic group/country of origin. With over seventeen million records, this collection is now considered the largest repository of first-person cultural data in the world.

Gathering a Brain Trust within the GEMI Scientific Community

2029

Throughout the 2020s, many leaders in academia and industry were critical of GEMI and, specifically, Dr. Jacob Baptista for poaching the best of the best scientific minds and talent to lead GEMI projects. They argued that this was the beginning of a decline in the quality of pure and applied research, not only in public and private higher education institutions worldwide, but also in government and private industries. In 2029, Cambridge, Stanford, Harvard, and MIT university systems published a joint statement in the *Journal for Higher Education*, denouncing these ongoing GEMI recruitments as "…a gross disregard for the larger scientific ecosystem, offering salaries and research budgets outside the limits of what most university systems can sustain. …" Indeed, by 2030, 112 Nobel Prize laureates had accepted research and teaching commitments within GEMI centers. During the same period, GEMI enticed more than 85,000 premier scientists and engineers from all disciplines to teach and train interns as they worked towards their research goals for GEMI.

A *New York Times* reporter asked Dr. Baptista why, as a respected scientist himself, he would go after these highly regarded scientists for GEMI — especially knowing he would be, to some degree, eroding the higher education institution of which he was a member for so long. He responded, "First, we have a mandate to get a very complex job done, and within an aggressive timeframe. We have the funding, and, frankly, we couldn't waste time prepping the personnel, hoping they were up to the task. And, of course, I wanted the best brains out there. I needed the best and most experienced professional scientists and engineers available. I needed their discipline-specific expertise and their ability to ramp up the research and development operations in their labs quickly and efficiently, with minimum oversight.

"Second, damn, come on. What we were offering them was exciting as hell — a once-in-a-lifetime opportunity — even at their rarefied levels of professional achievement. It's true that we've been competitive with compensation, but the real attraction is the project. We were giving them an opportunity to research and develop new, more efficient ways for humans to use or consume everything on Earth — energy, food, clothing, transportation, water, communications, health, infrastructure. Oh, yeah, and while you're at it, let's apply all this to living and traveling in space, and colonizing and terraforming Mars, too. And we were not always the instigators. Many scientists were knocking down our door for the chance to explore these opportunities."

By 2055, nearly six million interns had completed their five-year commitments and cycled through GEMI, gaining knowledge and work experience in a relevant scientific discipline from these world-class scientists and engineers. After returning to their country of origin, large numbers of these interns pursued advanced degrees related to their work in GEMI. With the valuable work experience garnered from their work/study in GEMI, others took professional positions in academia and industry. The high-caliber skills the interns demonstrated were widely recognized, and regardless of their university degree level, academia and industry have been quick to embrace them, affirming Dr. Baptista's decision to use top-tier scientists and engineers.

GEMI & IMPF — "We Can't Do It All"

The *Fisher Report* was thorough in its analysis of and recommendations for the environmental, financial, structural, and health-related systems around the world. As the project began to gain momentum, global leaders assumed that GEMI would endeavor to work on all of these recommendations. However, with the publication of the GEMI 20-point Project Roadmap, and Edward Fisher's city-based infrastructure investment strategy for IMPF, critics began to voice concern for what they felt was too narrow a focus — especially given the unprecedented level of funding for both projects. In September 2027, United Nations Secretary-General António Guterres issued a statement questioning GEMI's priorities: "With an unrestricted fund of $3.4 trillion, we had expected closer adherence to all recommendations in the *Fisher Report*. As well, there are many crises around the world deserving of some of these funds. We implore the GEMI leadership to loosen their grip on their cash reserves and help us to help the poorest among us."

Later that spring, GEMI CEO Dr. Hana Duarte responded to these criticisms during an interview with *Economics* magazine. She stated flatly, "We [GEMI] can't do it all. We have over 3,000 active scientific projects across our centers. We're following our roadmap, and we will not be bullied into doing more. In our opinion, this is how to dilute this effort — picking away at our funding and us losing our focus. It's not going to happen. With due respect for all the good things other organizations are doing, please allow us to follow our clearly stated mission."

Fisher addressed similar criticisms during the second annual IMPF shareholders meeting. Investors were becoming frustrated with IMPF's seeming inability to find enough investment opportunities to put their capital to work. Nearly two years since the fund's inception, there was still approximately $7 trillion — almost half — of the fund's capital still not committed to any project. This "dry powder" far exceeded what most experts considered wise cash management for an investment fund.

When confronted with this information and asked why the IMPF was not taking advantage of what was considered a bull market, Fisher explained the fund's focus was in developing crucial infrastructure systems for major cities across the world. He reiterated that IMPF supplied financing and general contractor-level project management strictly for large urban waste, water, energy, and transportation infrastructure projects.

"If we're able to retool these major infrastructure systems, we believe we can reach our stated carbon-neutral goals within the next thirty or so years. If we deviate and focus on just short-term returns, we will fail," Fisher said. "Do the math — if we can convert the top 100 most populous cities in the world to carbon-neutral, we have effectively taken care of the carbon footprints for about one billion people. That's more than one out of eight people in the world.

"We'll also have developed the expertise to roll this out to the rest of the world's thousands of cities. We'll be in a position to train the engineers attacking these challenges," Fisher continued. "This is the most efficient way for us to proceed with this fund. Don't worry — we'll be doing good works, and you'll still make a great return on your investment. We'll get there, but we won't be rushed. Just be patient."

First GEMI Space Colony Center Established

2029

One by one, during six weeks in November and December of 2028, GEMI, in partnership with pioneering artificial gravity colony company, Axiom Space[1], untethered seven co-developed Individual Space Habitats (ISHs) connected to the ISS. They attached each of them to the also-tethered first operational ISH hub via 56-meter-long pressurized spherical shafts. After two weeks of additional testing, the hub tether was removed on January 2, 2029, establishing the first GEMI space colony. This first self-contained and self-powered GEMI center community of ISHs was christened the Pleiades, or the Seven Sisters.

GEMI even named the seven ISHs after the mythical seven daughters of Atlas and Pleione, the protectress of sailing: Maia, Electra, Alcyone, Taygete, Asterope, Celaeno, and Merope. The hub was named Taurus after the astronomical constellation within which the Pleiades star cluster resides.

While Earthbound, Drs. Jacob Baptista and Hana Duarte were in virtual attendance for the inaugural launch. In his comments during the ceremony, Dr. Baptista noted, "Today, we have reached a key milestone for our GEMI space program. With assistance from our partners, Axiom Space and VAST, we have established both the first permanent, self-sustaining colony and the first GEMI center in space with the Pleiades. Personally, this colony gives me so much hope. With today's launch of the Pleiades Colony, we now have the means to live and work in LEO space colonies safely. This also gives us the capability and confidence to continue working towards one of our next big goals — the space elevator. We believe the space elevator is the gateway to living and working in space, and colonies like the Pleiades is where we'll live and work once this gateway is established."

This early ISH model could maintain life support systems for up to six people for two years. Although GEMI wanted the Pleiades to be a fully functional GEMI center, it was initially home to only forty-one scientists and interns due to space limitations, with another 2,000 Pleiades-assigned staff scattered through several Earth-bound centers. Those on Earth focused on projects much the same as if they were physically residing in the Pleiades.

GEMI routinely rotated Earth-bound and Pleiades-assigned scientists and interns for the next several years. Dr. Duarte explained the practicality of this method: "We have many goals for the Pleiades. One of them is normalizing the experience of living and working in space. So, we shuttle people to and from the Pleiades routinely. It's still unique, but we are all getting used to it. The Pleiades has only been operational for maybe three years now, and I have already been there twice."

Author's note: *The Pleiades Center has since grown considerably. In 2055, there were 53 ISHs interconnected through nine hubs in the center colony (including all seven sisters — still fully operational). The average Pleiades colony population (scientists, interns, and family members) numbers 300, with an additional 50 or so visitors in transit to and from other colonies or space projects.*

---

[1]GEMI invested capital and technical expertise in Axiom Space to complete the development of an operational artificial gravity colony. While GEMI did not "own" the Pleiades colony, they had an open-ended lease agreement commitment that is still active in 2055. However, as the owner of approximately one-third of Axiom, GEMI has

also been receiving ongoing revenue from the dozens of colonies Axiom has developed over the past twenty-five years.

First Patent and Beyond

2027

The successful ability to innovate is synonymous with long-term growth and stability for enterprises in almost all industries, and the development of intellectual property (IP) and patents are essential metrics of this success. By these measures, GEMI should thrive for a very long time.

No corporation has ever had such a clear mandate — and ample funding — to innovate as GEMI. From its inception, part of GEMI's mission was to do applied research and development across almost all industries to reduce humanity's negative impact on the environment. GEMI also sought to build enduring mechanisms to redistribute wealth throughout the world. One such mechanism was the careful management of GEMI-owned IP amassed through the decades.

GEMI was issued its first patent on February 18, 2027, for a simplified water purification system. The primary investigator, Dr. Julian Perez, and his team completed most of the work on this patent at the GEMI center in Velingrad, Bulgaria. A short twenty years later, in 2047, GEMI was awarded its 600,000th patent. This number has continued to grow, and by 2055, GEMI accounts for approximately 31% of the Patent Cooperation Treaty (PCT) patent applications submitted annually.

This dramatic increase illustrates the power of the hive-based[1] GEMI research foci, the substantial funding, the quality of the researchers and facilities, and above all, the leadership. The appointment of Dr. Baptista as Chief Science Officer was a significant factor. In a special report analyzing the GEMI intellectual property phenomena, *The Economist* wrote, "From the beginning, Dr. Baptista had a detailed road map for the development of the technologies necessary to meet the goals of GEMI — and the expertise to guide the effort. His scientific depth was and is unequaled, and, from early on, he also demonstrated an entrepreneur-like tenacity in pursuing dominance across most scientific domains. No wonder, worldwide, we have witnessed an exodus of the brightest scientific minds from business and academia to GEMI research centers, and the corresponding waning of cutting-edge intellectual property development outside of GEMI-influenced venues."

Most government and corporate leaders acknowledge they have saved hundreds of billions of dollars by licensing GEMI-owned technologies in lieu of attempting to develop the necessary technology with their own resources. However, GEMI has been criticized through the years for its growing IP dominance across many industries and for what critics considered excessive revenue generated from the licensing of this IP worldwide. In response to this criticism, Dr. Baptista once stated, "Our mission demands we do aggressive applied research and development across just about everything humans consume or use. And, of course, GEMI wants to maximize the returns on its IP. This is how we generate the dividends we disperse to our member countries. This stuff is all clearly stated in our charter."

Author's note: *Removing GEMI patent filings from the equation reveals another key phenomenon: Patent filings from low- to middle-income countries increased from 6% in 2030 to 45% in 2055, along with a corresponding decrease in filings for high-income countries from 94% to 55%. Many analysts attributed much of this dramatic increase in low-to middle-income country filings to the quality of GEMI interns' scientific training and work experience when they cycled through the research centers. Once interns return to their country of origin, they are almost invariably absorbed into either industry-based scientific and business positions or positions within university systems,* *leveraging their newfound knowledge and experience at home — thereby achieving yet another of GEM's original goals.*

———————————

[1]Proactive development of an interrelated "hive" of research data, ideas, and resources across a large and broad range of disciplines. Dr. Baptista explained, "I like to think of this as a small, creative, tightly knit research group of two million very smart, motivated researchers, all willing to share their individual research and, at a moment's notice, jump in to help with another unrelated project without hesitation. This concept is not a new one. And, yes, we use elements of AI to ensure we're all not inundated with mountains of information we cannot manage. But we've taken this to another level entirely. The whole process is transparent. Our budgeting and priorities are not subject to influence from the outcomes, either positive or negative. All we ask is that everyone — scientists, interns, janitors, everyone — enthusiastically participate. It was an easy sell."

The "Martians" Have Landed!

2029

Bill Stewart, a senior economic correspondent for the *New York Times*, used the phrase "Martians" in 2029 to describe the delegation of GEMI representatives (and, by inference, all GEMI personnel) meeting with the World Bank and United Nations officials in Adelaide, Australia. They were there to review the economic impact of GEMI on the regions of the world where centers were built. As expected, their findings showed that the resultant infusion of capital in these regions led to increased local prosperity, especially within poorer countries. However, this in turn increased migration from other areas into the regions hosting the centers, thereby stressing local infrastructures and governments. Leaders sought to relieve this stress by finding methods to diffuse the capital into other regions within their countries.

Stewart observed stark differences between the GEMI delegates and the bureaucrats from the World Bank and the U.N. He wrote, "As the Martians sauntered into the room, the other delegates scrutinized them with uncomfortable intensity, apparently feeling the vitality and power emanating from each of the GEMI representatives. The Martians' intelligence, restfulness, energy, and physical presence intimidated almost everyone in the room — me included. They were different somehow, as if they really could have been from Mars."

Dr. Hana Duarte responded with characteristic humor and deflection, stating, "Now, maybe some of us have gone off the deep end. We don't eat more than necessary to maintain our physical activity levels. We tend towards extremes — sports, intellectual pursuits — and consider it not only a challenge, but also a responsibility, to push our personal use of resources lower and lower. Still, I would argue that those Mr. Stewart referred to as 'Martians' are merely a subset of the GEMI population. We are not all quite that dedicated."

Often described as a melding of US Navy SEALs and Buddhist monks, with the intellect of MIT graduate students, these "Martians" are heads and shoulders above most of their contemporaries spread throughout the world. However, while many interns embrace the more extreme aspects of the GEMI philosophy of living, not all do so. Still, regardless of their responsibilities within GEMI, all interns are expected to participate in at least a moderately intense physical exercise regime while being educated and trained by the best minds in the world. If nothing else, almost all emerge from their five-year internship physically and mentally fitter.

The moniker "Martians," used to describe those working and learning within GEMI, endures to the present day. While these exceptional individuals wear this label with pride, most shrug off the elitist label, choosing instead to focus on using the tools they acquire at GEMI centers as they transition back to their home countries.

In 2055, GEMI alumni now number in the millions. They are enthusiastically involved in all levels in business, government, and academia, both here on Earth and in space. GEMI's unique, global blend of culture, coupled with focused technical skills immediately relevant to today's challenges and tomorrow's hopes, will continue to keep Martians in high demand as we enter the 2060s.

Let the Games Begin!

From its inception, GEMI cultivated a balanced blend of intellectual pursuits, physical prowess, and dietary health, wrapped within a teams-oriented framework among staff and interns alike. Dr. Hana Duarte recalled how the focus on high-caliber physical fitness began early in GEMI history.

"It started at our first center in Harrison, New Jersey. Dr. Baptista, of course, had their attention in the sciences. I mean, the science was bleeding edge across every discipline. That's why most of these young adults were there," she said. "Still, these were dynamic, high-energy people, and we had to engage them physically as well as intellectually — keep them busy and maybe a little exhausted by the end of the day. In Harrison, I used to organize runs, functional fitness workouts, MMA, rowing on the Passaic River — you name it.

"Also, I've always been interested in optimizing my diet — competition in sports will do that to you. Early on, I sort of transferred these habits to everyone as we moved forward with the project," Dr. Duarte continued. "Then, high achievers that most of us were, we started friendly competitions in these sports. It was a great way to ingrain fitness as a priority into the GEMI culture."

As the centers came online, Dr. Duarte instituted a comprehensive, standardized offering of sports across the centers, ensuring each had adequate facilities and equipment. As an active competitor in numerous sports, she then began encouraging ad hoc competitions among center athletes. These were so successful that in 2030, she introduced the first organized competition across all the centers, dubbed "The GEMI Games." Because of geographic challenges presented by CO_2 emissions limitations, most of the Games were held locally in the centers and broadcast in a virtual format.

GEMI carefully orchestrated the staging of each event, even introducing GEMI-developed holographic technologies in the early 2040s to give the athletes and spectators as close to an in-person experience as possible. For the few events requiring physical interactions between two competitors — such as MMA fighting — competitors would travel from centers worldwide to compete in person. Dr. Duarte, explaining how they did so in good global conscience, said, "Every center takes great pains throughout the year to accumulate carbon credits far above what's needed to offset any CO_2 emissions used to get athletes to the center hosting the Games each year – much easier now with emissions-free air travel."

In a 2047 documentary showcasing the GEMI Games, ESPN described the Games as essentially benign: "The GEMI Games are a mix of Olympic weightlifting, gymnastics, functional endurance tests, and martial arts-like competitions. These 'Martian' athletes are an intense group of individuals and teams, and most of them perform at the highest international level. While there are winners and losers, no money is involved. It is just about bragging rights."

Author's note: The yearly GEMI Games are still going strong in the late 2050s. While the events have evolved, they remain an eclectic mix of sports followed by tens of millions of GEMI peers and public spectators worldwide. Of particular note is how completely each center-hosting country has adopted its native center, cheering on their center's competitors with all the enthusiasm of proud parents cheering on their children.

Dividends Begin to Be Distributed

2031

In July 2031, for the first time, GEMI distributed a total of $275.54 billion in dividends to 122 countries, with each country receiving nearly $2.26 billion. Revenue contributing to this distribution came from $35 billion in sales and services worldwide (mostly patent licensing and consulting), and the remainder from realized profit from low-risk investment income in GEMI's master restricted funds account.

This dividend increased to $3.83 billion in 2035, and within a few years of the GEMI space elevator going into production in mid-2035, revenue from the shipping of material to and from space drove the annual dividends higher still. By 2040, the dividend had doubled to $7.90 billion per country.

Two other significant revenue contributors were GEMI-funded space colony systems and graphene space construction material. As space colonization accelerated in the late 2030s, GEMI's share of the sales of these systems and graphene-based materials, together with the continued increased use of the space elevator, pushed annual dividends even higher. In 2050, the payout had increased to $16.2 billion per country, rising to $22 billion in 2054.

While this number is relatively insignificant for the more affluent countries of the world, for the eighty or so countries with less than $150 billion in yearly GDP (2055 World Bank statistics), it amounts to a large infusion of capital. For those countries at the very bottom of the food chain, it accounts for up to 40% of their total yearly GDP. This stable, recurring annual revenue began to change the dynamic between such impoverished countries and the affluent countries and corporations to which they were historically beholden for irregular cash infusions laden with stipulations. Over time, these poorer countries have become more confident in guiding and funding their own destinies. This has been especially evident in the increased number of locally funded national and regional projects to rebuild natural resources previously used to meet short-term economic needs.

Ugandan President Bitalo Tumusiime affirmed this confidence in 2053, while addressing the U.N. Assembly on the efficacy of the GEMI model on the wealth of countries. "We [Ugandans] perceive the accumulation of wealth as many other countries do. Food, water, and shelter security, preservation of our natural resources and our culture, education for our young, hope for our future — these we consider wealth. And in these, our markers for success and wealth, we feel we have entered a golden age in Uganda. GEMI's internships for our youth through these past decades, and the annual dividends we earn, have undeniably contributed to this exciting new era. Why, we now even have Ugandans living and working in space colonies. Yes, the GEMI model works."

Baptista's Op-ed, "The Business of GEMI Science"

2036

By the early 2030s, detractors began to criticize GEMI, and Dr. Baptista specifically, for the lack of basic science initiatives and for the huge, risky financial outlays GEMI was willing to make through the years to ensure critical technologies were developed. In a June 2036 *New York Times* "Science" op-ed, Dr. Judith Lang, Director of the National Institutes of Health (NIH), lambasted Dr. Baptista and GEMI. She wrote, "Dr. Baptista and his group of 'manager scientists' are too focused on meeting deadlines — regardless of the cost — to reach their scientific milestones, eschewing tenets traditionally embedded within a scientific research institution. It is unconscionable and short-sighted for such a well-funded organization to turn a blind eye to the ongoing need for robust basic scientific research, while repeatedly gambling tens of billions of dollars on extremely risky projects."

The New York Times offered Dr. Baptista an opportunity to refute these claims. Baptista declined to respond directly but agreed to discuss, in essay format, his thoughts on the business of GEMI science. Below is the essay in its entirety.

"The Business of GEMI Science"

— Dr. Jacob Baptista, PhD, Chief Science Officer, GEMI

GEMI is in business to achieve clear, successive goals across an extraordinary spectrum of interrelated fields, here on Earth and in space, while maximizing and protecting annual dividends for our member countries. The scope of what we are attempting to accomplish is unprecedented — as is the funding (thank you, Edward Fisher). We are, essentially, attempting an epic, environmentally friendly "retooling" of just about everything we use, consume, and want to accomplish on Earth. Moreover, if that is not enough, we plan to colonize and eventually terraform Mars.

And who better than GEMI to take on these big, audacious, expensive goals? Not many entities — countries included — can assume the long-term financial risks nor have the expertise needed to realize many of these objectives. GEMI has a clear mandate to pursue our goals, free of oversight and with, arguably, adequate funding. Certainly, I, along with Dr. Hana Duarte and the GEMI community, recognize the enormous responsibility of being thoughtful stewards of this opportunity.

Our unique business model and funding allow Dr. Duarte and me autonomous use of our considerable financial and human resources to meet GEMI objectives. We are unencumbered by shareholders and a corporate board looking over our shoulders, delaying or stopping our progress by questioning our decisions. We also rely on a dense web of the highest caliber scientists, engineers, tradespeople, and interns living and working in our GEMI centers worldwide — a diverse team of over two million people. With this deep expertise, we can, with confidence, be bold, decisive, and nimble in our decision-making and execution of projects.

The ambitious work we are doing at our Earth-bound centers, is, frankly, more important in the short term than our work in space. Still, given what we are attempting to achieve in space, there are certain critical building blocks that must be in place to keep moving towards those objectives. What needs to be accomplished to colonize and terraform Mars? No one knows what unfathomable technologies will get us to that end game. Regardless, we needed first to develop a robust space ecosystem. So, what do we need in place to jump-start this space ecosystem?

To start, we need safe, fast, and inexpensive modes of transportation to get supplies and people to space. The best solution is a space elevator, which would transport supplies quickly and cheaply into lower Earth orbit. An elevator would help tremendously to supplement the hodgepodge of reusable multi-stage rockets and booster rocket-assisted spaceplanes already in use. However, until now, no existing material was strong enough for the space elevator cabling. No cabling means no elevator, and no elevator means a much slower development of the space ecosystem. So, we decided to develop the necessary super-strong graphene cabling — and the capability to make tens of thousands miles of it — and leveraged this knowledge to create graphene-based sheathing technologies for future spaceships and for colonies' infrastructures.

For mass human travel to and from space, we need reusable spaceplanes capable of safe take-off and landing at most standard airports. We also need safe habitats for people living and working in space for extended periods, which requires the establishment of artificial gravity-space colonies. With this in mind, and to have any chance of demonstrably moving closer to our Mars project objectives, we brought to life these critical components. We bet big on these technologies — and we still are.

Asteroid mining will be essential to self-sufficient space colonies and explorations, especially as we begin to move further from Earth. As such, this is one of GEMI's next critical investment areas: helping develop the technological foundation for mining resources from asteroids and from other planets. We plan to accomplish this with our recently formed partnerships with SpaceX, Exteriores Spartium Industries (ESI), and Ti'son Asteroid Corporation. These partners have experience building long-haul rockets, designing and constructing large space infrastructures, and landing on and mining asteroids. Together, we will develop the essential supply chain and transportation components needed to close the loop on this crucial space-based industrial channel.

We must continue executing the *State of the World Report*'s recommendations while carefully managing GEMI's human and financial resources. In doing so, we hope to satisfy the lofty goals of the GEMI charter while assisting in bringing humankind — both here on Earth and in space — into a new and enduring era of prosperity.

Author's note: *In response to a question during a scientific Q&A panel in 2035, Dr. Baptista responded to NIH Director Dr. Lang's 2034 New York Times comment, stating, "I emphatically agree with Dr. Lang on the importance of basic research. However, I postulate that we [GEMI scientists] do more basic research than most institutions precisely because we can focus on the end goal without regard to market pressures. We trust the value added will eventually reap profits by contributing to the knowledge base within one or more scientific fields and by meeting our goals. These profits are included in our annual dividend distributions to our member countries."*

GEMI Satellite Offices

2035

By 2030, the radius of influence began to increase for most GEMI centers worldwide. At first, the needs were simple, such as daycare services and nutritional counseling for locals working within the GEMI centers. However, the scope and breadth of community-requested services grew over time, and GEMI began opening satellite offices within the immediate vicinities of center locations.

These offices ranged from small storefronts to relatively large complexes within corporate and university settings. Dr. Duarte explained, "By this time, the communities where our centers were located had become our communities, too. We just began to fill gaps. It was a mix of services — small education and retraining centers, health clinics, food kitchens, housing projects for the homeless, new farming and green construction techniques, micro-business development — you name it. We even began opening community sports centers, which became a big hit."

By the early 2030s, with thousands of GEMI-sponsored satellite offices worldwide, Dr. Duarte added some structure to the satellites. She implemented budgets and systems to assist with programs and instituted an open-door policy similar to those found in centers, affording a level of transparency and trust. These offices focused entirely on the local population's needs and were managed chiefly by volunteer GEMI interns, GEMI alumni, and native professionals and tradespeople. The participation of interns and alumni guaranteed expertise and additional GEMI-based resources. Over time, these satellite locations would become a vital community resource, aiding tens of millions of individuals and families.

The willingness of GEMI interns to volunteer within their adopted local communities is almost legend. This phenomenon illuminated a significant difference between GEMI centers and the university systems to which they have often been compared. Within GEMI, interns are not tested in the traditional sense. They are expected to study to understand their field and apply their training to take on work assignments. However, they are not subject to periodic quantitative testing to measure and rank their mastery of a subject, thereby resulting in significantly more free time. As they became accustomed to altruistically working within extended groups, they naturally became involved in these local communities.

Annually, from 2030 to the present, having completed their five-year tour within GEMI, upwards of 1,000 interns are rotated back into their country of origin. Most of these are absorbed into their country's education and business ecosystems. However, many take short-term, low-paying positions at one of their country's GEMI satellite locations, building expertise in their chosen field while working with the local GEMI center to implement community programs.

The organic growth of these busy satellite offices was not devised by GEMI but was driven entirely by the practical needs of the local population. This quiet willingness, over decades, of the volunteers to become valuable and trusted members of their adopted community, more than any other factor, contributed to the long-term success of GEMI.

Author's note: *As of the writing of this book, there are approximately 15,000 GEMI satellite office locations worldwide, with an average of fifty staff members per location. Every country in the world hosts at least one GEMI satellite office, regardless of whether they host a GEMI center.*

Baptista and His Models

2036

In addition to his other accolades, Dr. Baptista is also considered a "master engineer" in that he actively participates in the physical designs and implementations of his wide range of inventions. Even in his youth working for scientists at the Los Alamos Labs, Dr. Baptista would build physical models of his ideas (and the ideas of others) on his family's ranch to help him more fully understand concepts and bring them to fruition. He would continue creating models throughout his tenure with GEMI.

Dr. Baptista explained this bent towards working with his hands in his autobiography: "It gives me great pleasure to physically create something out of nothing. If it's in my mind — say, some obscure theorem or hypothetical widget — it helps me somehow to work through what's left to accomplish by physically building a model of whatever it is I dreamed up. I get deep, visceral satisfaction from these activities."

During an interview with Dr. Duarte, she described Dr. Baptista's handiwork early in the GEMI project. She had recently accepted the CEO position and had arrived at the first center, located in an abandoned industrial complex on the East River in Harrison, New Jersey in the United States — the center she would consider her home base for the next thirty years. She spoke of her first encounter with Dr. Baptista's models:

"What hit me were these enormous models. I had no clue, but apparently Jacob was already famous for the models he built to help him develop his ideas. So, anyway, that first morning, Jacob was waiting for me at the shipping dock entrance to the warehouse he had commandeered as his headquarters. He hands me a cup of coffee — 'good morning, welcome to GEMI, nice day, blah, blah' — and then we walk into this massive space, sort of like an indoor horse arena.

"And there they were, these colossal models. I just stood there staring. I didn't know what they were at first. I mean, we were just ramping the project up, but Jacob already had the basics of a few of what would be GEMI's biggest inventions in model form. The space elevator was extended from the floor to the rafters, at least fifty feet up. You could climb through the middle right up to the top! A large Earth sphere — it had to have been at least thirty feet in diameter — had most of the center locations already identified on its skin. He even had a basic 3-ISH / hub colony hanging from the rafters. They were big. I have no idea how he got them up there. Very similar to the eventual real deal — uncanny. Wood, scrap metal, wire — you name it, he used it to put these models together." Shaking her head, Duarte continued, "And his three horses were grazing on hay flakes on the ground below. It was kind of surreal.

"He took me up to the colony model to finish our coffee and talk. We had to climb the ladder in the elevator to a top platform. He had a pulley system set up to pull the colony cluster to the elevator. He secured a cable from one of the ISHs to the elevator; we stepped over and into the ISH, and he released the cable. We swung gently for a few minutes and then stabilized. It was all chicken wire wrapped around wood and metal framing, with some sections boxed in with sheet metal. He had cardboard components in the living quarter areas and even mock-ups of the life-sustaining apparatus.

"Jacob explained how immersion in these models was important to him when working through the design and development of his ideas and those of the other scientists. We were up there for maybe two hours discussing the project and its future. He was right, I could feel the energy and creativity flowing — we were truly in it. I can't tell you how many times we found him sleeping in an ISH, or climbing up and down the elevator, or simply staring at something he had recently put together — occasionally stopping to take notes, wave, or whatever."

Author's note: *More than 1,000 of Dr. Baptista's models are on display at the GEMI Library and Museum on the grounds of the Tiras Mountains, Namibia Center (TNc).*

GEMI and the Martian Philosophy Embraced around the World

2055

Coined by the media in the late-2020s, the tongue-in-cheek moniker "Martians" initially poked fun at the characteristics of most of the employees, interns, and alumni of GEMI and their audacious Mars project. However, while the term stuck, the meaning morphed into a description of the unique blend of intellectual acuity, physical prowess, and cultural norms shared by most GEMI personnel — and envied and emulated by millions of people worldwide.

Most individuals associated with GEMI embrace all that being Martian entails without jeopardizing any of their core values. This duality, above all else, enabled Martian philosophy to flourish around the world. Allen Borg, the United Nations Secretary-General from 2037-2041, once poetically described the subtle GEMI influences within societies worldwide as "a gossamer veil descending on one's core belief system, enhancing the whole without diminishing."

But why are GEMI and the Martians almost universally admired by people and embraced (or at least tolerated) by most governments, religions, and cultures of the world? Many cultural anthropologists give at least partial credit to the unique development of the GEMI culture, which while it has taken on a life of its own over the last three decades, has derived its norms from hundreds of local cultures around the world.

This adaptation, the anthropologists argue, offers something familiar for almost all cultures. In essence, the familiarity inherently reduces the fear and tension commonly experienced between a local society and what they may have otherwise interpreted as an interloper.

Political scientists have noted another significant factor in GEMI's popular appeal: the organization's extreme level of transparency, upon which Dr. Duarte insisted to protect GEMI's integrity. A 2041 *Perspectives on Politics* article, "Influential International Non-Profit Organizations in Local Political Systems," stated, "The utter transparency that permeates the entire [GEMI] organization, some have argued, is at best naive. However, any international organization simply claiming no political or religious affiliation does not work in today's cynical world. GEMI's open-book policy quickly takes the steam out of any accusations from local political or religious leaders. They are always free to audit their centers and satellite offices, albeit at their own expense."

Another compelling reason for the acceptance of GEMI is money. The 2055 IMF World Financial Statement reported that eighty-two countries received dividend payments from GEMI totaling more than 15% of their GDP in the previous year. Nearly 100 countries host GEMI centers, and there are approximately 15,000 GEMI satellite offices spread throughout every country in the world. Yearly recurring revenue from the scientific and administrative operations of all centers and satellite offices approaches $750 billion. Factoring in a carefully managed multiplier effect means GEMI's presence around the world is worth upwards of $2.8 trillion annually for the local economies — on top of the annual dividend payments made to all participating countries.

Dr. Duarte gave her opinion as to why GEMI and the Martian philosophy are embraced around the world. "It's all about trust. Over time, local communities and countries saw we had no hidden agenda. We asked each country for permission to build a center within their borders. We made long-term financial commitments — fifty-year leases for most of our center facilities — and we worked with local contractors and merchants to build out the centers," she said. "Over time, we slowly became part of each local community. We became stewards of these communities, and they saw our generosity and our sincere commitment to them. Citizens, governments, and religious organizations saw how we respected their local heritage and culture. We laugh, cry, work, and live alongside them."

Hana Duarte's Retirement Interview

When I began to write this history, I had no idea Dr. Hana Duarte was within months of announcing her retirement as the CEO of GEMI, a position she held for nearly thirty years. Shortly after the announcement, I asked her if she would be willing to do an interview focusing on her accomplishments during her tenure with GEMI for inclusion in this historical account. Duarte agreed to a short interview but — just as with this history — with conditions. She wanted to wait until the history was in final draft form and she had an opportunity to review it. I suspect she wanted to ensure we did not discuss something already covered. As I have learned during the last two years of working with Dr. Duarte, she dislikes wasted time and redundancies. She was (and still is) frugal and efficient.

Also (and to my point above), she did not want to focus on what she accomplished while CEO of GEMI. She told me that if I did my job, all of that would be covered within the history. She wanted to focus on the future, and she wanted to keep it short. Again, as with her conditions for the history, I acquiesced.

Below is the transcript of the interview.

Author: Dr. Duarte, first, thank you so much for your unwavering support during the past two years. Also, for agreeing to do this interview. It's the perfect capstone for the history.

Duarte: You're welcome. How would you like to begin?

Author: Let's jump right in. For the last thirty years, you've been the CEO of an organization attempting to achieve a complex set of objectives, involving over a hundred research and development centers in almost as many countries, and in space. You manage millions of interns, scientists, and workers, and have a budget in the hundreds of billions of dollars. You are admired, respected, and emulated by millions around the world, and are widely credited with having laid the groundwork for many of the societal changes that have occurred during this period. The GEMI "Martian" culture and the emergence of regionalism, to name just two, are movements you're closely associated with. With due respect, how did a Vassar College professor — with no business experience — accomplish so much in only thirty years?

Duarte: Well, Edward Fisher selected me because of my expertise in certain fields — and my inexperience in others. I must confess, much of what we accomplished was already laid out in the *State of the World Report* [aka, the *Fisher Report*] back in 2024. I've simply been working through a very long, very detailed to-do list for the last thirty years. There were many surprises and challenges, of course. Many. But, as individuals and as a global organization, we worked our way through them all — a team of millions. What I accomplished during the last thirty years hopefully validated Fisher's decisions. I just did my job.

Author: What has GEMI meant to you personally?

Duarte: As both a human being and a cultural anthropologist, I've been blessed in my relationship with the GEMI organization. Because of GEMI, I've been immersed in hundreds of cultures, interacting directly or indirectly with probably millions of individuals. I've been on the front lines of major societal and environmental changes here on Earth — and, in space, the development and expansion of space colonization. I've been a worker and witness to arguably one of the greatest, most creative, and productive periods in human history. What a wonderful backdrop for a life.

Author: Thank you, Doctor. Now, I agreed to keep this short, so: What does the future hold for GEMI here on Earth and in space?

Duarte: On Earth, GEMI will continue to thrive as a benevolent leader in society and technology. Most of the world is slowly shifting priorities from CO_2 emission reductions to a more routinized use of renewable energy sources, and GEMI is deeply involved in this transition. I also think GEMI centers will continue to thrive quietly within their host communities, ensuring the mission of GEMI remains intact.

In space, we're still in our infancy. We'll continue to witness an exodus of people to space colonies — probably for many decades to come. And I'm certain GEMI will continue to participate in space colonization and exploration. Remember, we still haven't terraformed Mars yet.

Author: And for you? What does the future hold for you in retirement?

Duarte: Well, I'm going to spend time with my family in Paraguay for the first few months. And, of course, I'll continue to lecture at the university level, especially on cultural anthropology. I still find it fascinating. But I'll also begin research for a book I plan to write exploring space colonization and its implications for societal and cultural changes. I'll visit several colonies as part of my research. I'm very excited about that. I mean, what an opportunity to closely examine space-based societies first-hand early in their development.

Author: Let's see if I remember from your lecture series. "Participant observation," right?

Duarte: Yes, yes — correct. I'm working with the United Space Colonies Collaborative[1] to coordinate extended visits to at least six colonies, including Hubbard's sprawling mining colony in the

Jupiter trojan asteroid region. It's one of the oldest deep-space colonies. There are over 1,200 individuals living there who have been in space continuously for ten-plus years. It's a once-in-a-lifetime opportunity for an anthropologist. I'm very lucky.

Author: Wow — that *is* exciting. Will you visit one of GEMI's colonies? And how long will you be in space?

Duarte: No, I'm not planning to visit any of the GEMI colonies — at least not for this purpose. For how long, I'm not sure yet. It depends on which colonies I visit. Certainly three or four years, maybe longer.

Author: So, will you continue your sport competitions? They seem to be a big priority for you.

Duarte: Ha, yes, of course! I'm very much looking forward to the upcoming virtual GEMI Games[2]. The events are always meticulously designed and tough, and the competition is always getting better. And, anyway, I love the act of physical conditioning. I'll continue to train regardless — it's a habit and a pleasure.

Author: One last question. Will you be involved in the leadership of GEMI going forward? I know you hand-selected Dr. Alisha Sapra as your replacement. Will you assist her? Or consult, maybe?

Duarte: No. Just like Fisher before us, Dr. Baptista and I will have no say in any GEMI decisions or business matters after each of us retires. The GEMI charter clearly states the transition protocol: All ties must be cut between outgoing leadership and GEMI. Dr. Baptista retired three years ago, and I will as well in a few months. At that point, Dr. Sapra will become the CEO, just as Dr. Zofia Jankowski became CSO [Chief Science Officer] when Dr. Baptista left. It's important for the organization. The world keeps changing, and GEMI must have strong, young leaders not tied to any dogmas from the past. You know, as we age, we cannot help but get a little sticky in our beliefs. That's not healthy for GEMI.

Author: Dr. Duarte, thanks again for your time today. I am so looking forward to watching what you do next.

Author's note: After three decades leading GEMI, Dr. Hana Duarte's steadfast integrity, physical, spiritual, intellectual vitality, and guileless nature have left an indelible mark on GEMI and the world. She, more than any other, embodies the moniker "Martian." To this day, I cannot help but think of Dr. Duarte as from out of this world — the very first Martian.

---

[1]Founded in 2044, the United Space Colonies Collaborative (USCC) is a non-affiliated space-based umbrella organization representing approximately 70% of the registered space colonies (as of 2055). USCC coordinates traveling to/from colonies and facilitates the community development of various inter-colony policies and procedures.

[2]The GEMI Games utilize virtual immersion presentations to ensure fair competition regardless of the location of each competitor.

INFRASTRUCTURE MEGA-PROJECT FUND (IMPF)

Edward Fisher's special-purpose global investment/project management fund had an enormous positive impact on our tenuously successful battle against global warming. Fisher founded IMPF to focus a substantial portion of our global investment capital towards reducing urban CO_2 emissions worldwide. He also had the foresight to create a mechanism that would gracefully dissolve IMPF when the need to maximize investments in space-related enterprises was at a critical juncture.

IMPF Described

2025

Edward Fisher founded the Infrastructure Mega-Project Fund (IMPF) in 2025. Defined as a socially responsible fund, IMPF had a narrow investment mandate. Its mission was to develop and execute large, complex urban infrastructure projects to help meet time-sensitive international goals to reduce CO_2 emissions — while providing an acceptable return for its investors. IMPF supplied financing and general contractor-level project management and engineering guidance for large urban waste, water, energy, and transportation infrastructure projects. The fund initially focused on mega-infrastructure projects within the hundred most densely populated cities worldwide. Fully funded at $14 trillion in 2028, at its peak, IMPF reported total assets of $76 trillion (IMPF 2047 annual report).

Shortly after announcing the establishment of the fund, Fisher said, "You know, it is in our nature to make a profit from most of our endeavors. While the fund might be considered — and rightly so — to be somewhat altruistic, it is still an investment tool. Just think of IMPF as a healthy relief valve for the world's investors. I created IMPF to specifically fund and manage infrastructure projects that will help bring densely populated mid- and large-sized urban environments down to zero-carbon footprints, and then model these various projects to be successfully replicated across most urban centers. We are helping with the global remedial grunt work needed to reach our goal of reducing human-generated emissions of carbon dioxide to net zero by 2050. We are laser-focused on this, and IMPF, as a private investment company with a large amount of capital and expertise, can make decisions and act in ways government-funded projects cannot.

"This work could never have been accomplished within GEMI. GEMI needs to focus all its resources on research and development, not funding and managing mega-projects worldwide. It is too expensive and risky, and frankly, the expertise is not there. It just would not have been prudent to subject the participating nations, or the GEMI operating funds, to the financial stress and risk associated with each project. GEMI needs the funding to meet its short- and long-term goals — one of which is for the participating countries, over time, to realize revenue from the services and patents GEMI research will generate. We do not want to jeopardize any of this income flow."

Another significant IMPF commitment — and a big boost for the cities partnering with IMPF — was the requirement of each sub-contractor to utilize local labor and materials whenever possible. IMPF project managers monitored and enforced this stipulation very closely. This careful management of resources resulted in a large infusion of additional revenue for participating cities due to the realization of the enhanced multiplier effect.

IMPF worked closely with each city to quantify this ongoing return. As of 2055, the average capital multiplier effect across three decades and more than 1,650 projects was twenty-three times the initial project investment — far exceeding the three to eight times typically realized in more passive mega-projects.

Author's note: Up until 2047, when it was announced IMPF would dissolve its services, the fund had maintained the status of the largest investment fund in the world, with $76 trillion in assets. In addition, IMPF had, at that time, completed 1,673 mega-projects across nearly every country in the world.

Why Both GEMI and IMPF?

2027

During the funding period for GEMI and IMPF, confusion and concern arose from many quarters, especially as accumulated funding reached the trillions. Was IMPF an extension of GEMI? Did investors somehow "own" GEMI by default once they had invested in the IMPF fund? Wasn't this, in some form, a conflict of interest? Edward Fisher at first refused to respond formally to these queries from government, business, and financial leaders. However, at the invitation of the *Wall Street Journal* in 2027, Fisher wrote an op-ed explaining the corporate structures of both organizations and the rationale behind keeping them separate.

An excerpt from the op-ed reads: "When I decided to move ahead with the GEMI project, IMPF was not part of the plan. However, as we worked through the budget for GEMI, we were stuck on how to substantively contribute to reaching the net-zero CO_2 emissions goal within GEMI proper. Rebuilding the world's infrastructures to meet the CO_2 emission reduction goals within the timeframe most scientists agreed on was far more complex than we first imagined, and we estimated it would cost five times more than all the other GEMI goals combined.

"Ultimately, we decided to create a second organization to focus solely on the infrastructure projects. Remember, GEMI is a significant non-profit research and development entity with a broad humanitarian mandate that includes substantial long-term financial commitments to its member nations. There will be thousands of city-based infrastructure projects, all highly complex, each demanding large capital commitments and having significant financial risks. These risks are best assumed by investors who understand and accept the real possibility of losing money in their quest to make an acceptable return on their investments. These types of risks do not belong in GEMI.

"In contrast, the IMPF we envisioned and founded is a standard investment vehicle for individual and institutional investors. IMPF is already a large organization, and I understand entirely why this makes government and business leaders uncomfortable. However, it does have a specific mandate: supply the financing and manage strategically targeted, city-based infrastructure projects, with the goal of reducing CO_2 emissions worldwide while making a decent return for investors. There are no other agendas.

"The management and financial structures of both entities are transparent and entirely separate. While I was intimately involved in the initial funding and development of both GEMI and IMPF, I only have leadership responsibilities within IMPF. As frustrating as it is to me at times, I do not have any influence in the management of GEMI. Drs. Duarte and Baptista lead the two arms of GEMI, and, in my opinion, they are doing a great job. I am the CEO of IMPF. This is my only responsibility."

While the op-ed succeeded in placating the detractors, it was the ongoing and unprecedented level of business and financial transparency that thwarted subsequent attacks on the corporate integrity of GEMI and IMPF. Both entities were always, literally, open books.

Fisher Defends the Creation of IMPF

2028

IMPF and GEMI were richly funded, with an unprecedented combined worth of over $17 trillion in 2028. To put it in perspective, this amount exceeded the 2028 GDP of every country in the world except the United States ($35.32 trillion) and China ($31.13 trillion). While there were a few investment funds at the time with several trillions of dollars under management, they were diverse funds regulated within various international financial markets. In contrast, both IMPF and GEMI were privately held corporations, and, as such, were relatively free of the controls governing publicly held companies.

This concerned world leaders. They were worried about the potential impact of $17 trillion in committed investment capital on the world economy — especially in the hands of just two private companies guided by CEOs many considered rogue. IMPF CEO Edward Fisher, while a respected businessman, had a reputation as an aggressive entrepreneur. The GEMI co-CEOs, on the other hand, were Dr. Hana Duarte, an unknown academic with no management experience, and Dr. Jacob Baptista, an eccentric Noble Prize–winning scientist.

Retired U.N. Secretary-General António Guterres voiced the concerns of many of his peers at the time. "The world was still recovering from three years of a devastating pandemic. Globally, most countries were in dire straits — and we were all gearing up for the serious climate work that was picking up steam," he said. "It was a lot of money, and there were too many ways Mr. Fisher's grand experiment could utterly fail."

In April of 2028, Fisher was called before a special session of the U.S. Securities Exchange Committee (SEC) to explain the rationale for creating IMPF, as opposed to doing this work within GEMI; to clarify the relationship between IMPF and GEMI; and to describe the leadership structure of both corporations. Below is a partial transcript of his testimony.

U.S. Senator Marco Rubio (R-FL), SEC Committee Chair: "Mr. Fisher, please describe the purpose of IMPF to the committee."

Edward Fisher: "Purpose? Well, the stated mission of IMPF is to help maximize long-term global CO_2 reductions by supplying the financing and managing transportation, energy, and waste infrastructure projects for major urban centers around the world, while realizing a healthy return for our investors."

Rubio: "But why such a narrow focus? And why cities around the world? Why not focus on cities in the United States? Surely, we can use trillions of dollars in funding for our own infrastructure."

Fisher: "Senator, this is by no means a narrow focus. Within the next several years, we will initiate projects for a hundred targeted mega-cities in almost that many countries. Collectively, this impacts about a quarter of the world's population, and our research predicts this work will dramatically reduce CO_2 emissions for these cities."

Rubio: "Okay, noted. So, was it a coincidence that you founded the GEMI project and then IMPF within a year of each other?"

Fisher: "Of course not. They're related. As we were developing the action plan to meet the recommendations of the *State of the World Report*, it became clear we needed a lot more money and a focus on remediating the infrastructures for the densest urban centers in the world. There was no way GEMI could be expected to accomplish that, along with all its other goals. And the price tag was far greater than the funding we collected for GEMI."

Rubio: "So, Mr. Fisher, you thought you could create a second entity [IMPF] and then oversee both?"

Fisher: "No, Senator. GEMI and IMPF are autonomous, and I have no authority in GEMI. Dr. Hana Duarte, as Chief Executive Officer, oversees administration, and Dr. Jacob Baptista, as Chief Science Officer, oversees research and development. I legally handed over the reins to them within days of their taking the positions. IMPF, on the other hand, is a different story. I'm the CEO, so other than occasionally butting heads with the Board of Directors, I have the final say in everything.

"Look, we did the math and had the difficult conversations. We chose the best way we could substantively assist in the global reduction of CO_2 emissions. We needed to quantify, and then accept, the global scale of the job we needed to do to have any chance of meeting our long-term goal of carbon neutrality by 2050. The only way we saw this maybe working was to incorporate a for-profit organization, raise the necessary capital, and get to work.

"IMPF will eventually help hundreds of large cities worldwide become carbon-neutral, and we'll make our investors money. Also, through careful management of the contracts and processes within each project, we expect to realize large multiplier effects in these local economies. We'll also develop best practices in urban infrastructure to use in thousands of smaller city centers worldwide. Senator, this is a win-win for all involved."

Author's note: The autonomy of IMPF and GEMI was challenged often through the 2020s and 2030s. Most notable was the failed attempt in 2037, by the International Monetary Fund (IMF), to build an international coalition of government, business, and religious leaders and coerce IMPF into relinquishing control to IMF. Similar in intent was the nearly successful United Nations 2042 bid to absorb GEMI into existing U.N. programs. Both attempts were thwarted by grassroots efforts within the IMF Board of Governors and by U.N. members.

IMPF: Too Much Cash!

2029

By 2028, only three years after Edward Fisher launched the fund, IMPF had successfully reached its designated fund investment goal of $14 trillion[1]. Fisher made the announcement in February, lauding the far-reaching generosity and stewardship of the investors buying into what he described as "…a fund with a goal damn near as audacious as GEMI's goal of terraforming and colonizing Mars."

A short thirteen months later, during an ad hoc stockholder call, Fisher made another announcement. IMPF, while fully funded, was facing the unique challenge of having too much unused capital on hand — approximately $7.6 trillion. Fisher stated that while this "dry powder" was not the ideal use of these funds, IMPF would continue to take the necessary time to research and plan each project carefully. He reminded everyone of the fund's mission: to protect their investments and, through the successful completion of the projects they fund, "move us towards our shared global goal of a carbon-neutral world."

Fisher again addressed the issue at the 2029 IMPF annual shareholders meeting, stating: "As most of you are aware, our goal of accumulating $14 trillion for our fund war chest was not arbitrary. In broad strokes, we estimated that each of the initial projects would cost an average of $100 billion or so. Doing the math, we needed upwards of $10 trillion in working capital to execute these projects, each of which takes years to complete. Do a little more math, and we needed a substantial buffer to sustain the business until completed projects begin to fill our coffers again. Add another $4 trillion.

"Remember, these are incredibly complex projects, but we're already becoming more efficient in working with the city- and country-level officials to get through each project's legal and financial issues, designs, and timelines. We expect to have a full portfolio of active projects in the works within the next two years. We've already identified all the target cities and the general project mix for each, but we need to be very careful in doing our homework for each project.

"We're also acutely aware of the larger picture and what that means now, in 2029. We are part of the solution to reduce CO_2 emissions to net zero by 2050. We must move on these projects as quickly as possible. Every day counts. Still, we will be careful with every penny we spend. We will not be pressured into beginning projects prematurely."

As of Fisher's shareholder meeting comments, nineteen projects were already active. By 2040, of the 100 targeted cities, thirty-four projects were still active and sixty-six had been completed. By 2045, with credit to Fisher's tenacity and IMPF project leadership, all but three of the one hundred initial active projects[2] had been completed. The three incomplete projects were temporarily derailed during the 2040-43 conflict between Pakistan and India, when the New Delhi project and the two Karachi projects were suspended because of sporadic bombing in both cities. Both Karachi projects resumed in 2044 and were completed in 2047. The New Delhi project resumed in 2045 and was completed in 2048.

---

[1]Much of the investments were multi-year commitments of increasing capital for bonds to finance cities across the world for their infrastructure projects.

[2]While Fisher measured IMPF success based mostly on the one hundred projects he and Dr. Baptista had originally identified, IMPF successfully completed hundreds of urban infrastructure projects before its dissolution in the early 2050s.

An Early IMPF
Mega-Project

2032

One of the first city mega-projects IMPF executed was Mexico City. With approximately 22 million inhabitants in the Greater Mexico City region, this was one of the world's most densely populated metropolises. In addition, its general infrastructure was built over centuries and was never meant to sustain millions of inhabitants. Decades-long accelerated urbanization, transportation congestion, poor air quality, lack of potable water, and inadequate waste removal systems, resulting in dangerous overpopulation, were daily struggles of the local government and citizens.

By 2020, Mexican leadership had published an aggressive plan to rebuild most of its urban infrastructure components over ten years. The Mexican Cities Initiative of the early 2020s was a collection of more than 150 small and large projects estimated to ultimately cost investors and the public sector almost 2.5 trillion pesos ($124 billion US).

Shortly after IMPF was founded in 2025, Mexico's new President, Claudia Sheinbaum Pardo, reached out to Edward Fisher to explore how IMPF might be able to assist in Mexico City's plans. Eventually, they agreed to engage IMPF in four large projects:

- The creation of a new 30,000-acre urban park/water reservoir
- The modernization of the public transportation systems (highways, railways, and ports of entry into the city)

- The design and construction of a new waste management system
- The modernization of the entire energy grid

IMPF supplied $91 billion US in financing and managed all four projects.

IMPF contracted with the U.S. Department of Energy's Environmental System Science Data Infrastructure for a Virtual Ecosystem (ESS-DIVE) to quantify the CO_2 impact of each of the Mexico City projects. Before project launch, ESS-DIVE developed a baseline for each component and then remeasured CO_2 emissions two years after project completion. Relative to the baseline, ESS-DIVE estimated Mexico City reduced its overall yearly CO_2 emissions by 47% in 2035. Total emissions reductions are categorized as follows:

- Transportation: 61%
- Energy efficiency: 14.2%
- Carbon sequestration by reforestation / urban park-related: 12.7%
- Waste management: 12.1%

In a joint statement commemorating the completion of the IMPF projects in 2032, Pardo praised Fisher and IMPF's involvement in the projects and their success. "Mr. Edward Fisher and his company have shown how a hybrid investment/management company can aid urban governments in meeting global goals surrounding the reduction of CO_2 emissions, while greatly improving the quality of life for those living and working within our borders. In addition to completing each of these large, complex projects on budget and on time, IMPF leadership's careful management of project funding resulted in impressive multiplier effects. To date, we estimate these projects have infused over two times the capital spent on the projects into local and regional economies. This amounts to 4.1 trillion pesos ($198 billion US). We fully expect to reap the benefits of this careful financial stewardship for many years to come."

IMPF Hits \$35 Trillion in Investments

2036

The Infrastructure Mega-Project Fund (IMPF) hit \$35 trillion in total investments and cash by the end of the calendar year 2036. To put this in some perspective, the fund exceeded, by nearly \$1 trillion, all Sovereign Wealth Funds (SWFs) worldwide and equaled 16% of the world's Gross Domestic Product (GDP) for the same period (approximately \$220 trillion). While there were a handful of global funds in the \$5 trillion to \$15 trillion range in existence at the time, IMPF was twice the size of its largest competitor fund and dominated the urban infrastructure industry worldwide.

Speaking at the September 2036 United Nations General Assembly meeting in New York City, IMPF CEO Edward Fisher downplayed the size and the influence of the fund on business around the world, stating, "We've been in a sustained growth mode for over a decade — since day one, really. We established our investment strategy and mission early on, and we do not plan on deviating from this path. Yes, we're larger than most other companies, at least in the capital we have under management. But we are somewhat benign in that we're narrowly focused on large infrastructure projects within mid-sized to large cities worldwide.

"But the capital — we have to have it. I mean, a typical city infrastructure project will cost anywhere between a few billion dollars to hundreds of billions. This amount of capital invested over the life of each project necessitates an enormous capital reserve. Just as an example, last year [calendar year 2035] IMPF was the principal underwriter for 436 active projects. Of these, the cost of each of the top hundred projects averaged roughly $75 billion, or $7.5 trillion in total. Add in the other 300-odd projects for another $15 trillion. So, IMPF was responsible for almost $23 trillion in active projects last year. During the same period, we completed ninety-one projects worldwide, worth approximately $7.8 trillion — money trickling back into our coffers."

When asked how long he thought IMPF would experience this level of growth, Fisher responded, "Over the last eleven years, we've aggressively pursued the largest, messiest infrastructure projects worldwide — those with historically the greatest CO_2 emissions, and so the greatest potential for CO_2 reductions. Overall, we're meeting our goals, and we've learned a lot about what works and what does not.

"We — all of us — now need to push to retool the infrastructures of not only the larger urban environments of the world, but also the smaller cities and even down into towns and micro-communities. Our expertise is still very much in demand, but we cannot do this alone. Two years ago, we began to template the best practices surrounding redesigning and developing the most environmentally impactful city infrastructure components.

"We have been working closely with businesses and governments to disseminate this knowledge. With their assistance, we believe we can still see substantial gains in reducing CO_2 emissions worldwide. We figure this will slow the growth of IMPF, but we'll be building a broader foundation of businesses with expertise in the related industry verticals. In my opinion, these additional resources will help us meet the global CO_2 emission reduction goals we have collectively set for 2050. These are time-sensitive goals we have all agreed are critical to meet."

IMPF and the Multiplier Effect

The focus on maximizing the multiplier effect was one of the most significant contributors to the success of the IMPF projects. The concept of a multiplier effect (ME) had been a known phenomenon in economics for decades. However, for both Edward Fisher and Dr. Jacob Baptista, the passive multiplier effects of a large capital infusion within a region were only the beginning.

Dr. Baptista's scientific paper, "Theoretical Limits of the Multiplier Effect in Regional Economies," was published in the *Journal of Macroeconomics* in 2013 and recognized through his Nobel Prize in Economics in 2028. In the paper, he made the basic assumption that the ME, in most localized occurrences, was a passive process with less-than-optimal returns. He demonstrated that the theoretical limits of the ME — in a tightly controlled environment over a period of twenty years — approached a factor of thirty times that of allowing a ME to grow passively over the same period.

Fisher believed in Dr. Baptista's work, and together they developed a computer system they could use to optimize this phenomenon. Fisher then mandated that all IMPF projects be managed within the framework of the model. GEMI would also adopt this model for its center development and ongoing R&D activities.

The disciplined use of the model, especially on such a large scale, dramatically demonstrated that large infusions of capital in a region could multiply up to thirty times over an extended period, instead of the five to eight times a passive approach would typically yield. As well, the passive use of the ME would generally dwindle within five years. Careful use of the Baptista model both intensified the effect and prolonged the life of the phenomena — often to twenty years or more.

Teams carefully collected data before the beginning of each IMPF project, including the measurement of relevant environmental and demographic markers and the cash flowing in/out of the region where the project would be executed. This data served as a baseline from which they were able to measure the project's efficacy across both the broader environmental goal of reducing CO_2 emissions and any increase in the fundamental economic health of the region. The consistent success of this ME model has led to its adoption across numerous industries and governments worldwide.

For IMPF, each project was indeed a partnership with the local community. As projects were completed and data collected, cities and countries began to realize the added value in partnering with IMPF. Unlike most multinational conglomerates of the time, IMPF worked with each city to ensure they were prepared to maximize the newly implemented systems, and the ME, for as long as possible.

Edward Fisher's Last Interview

2036

On March 21, 2037, Edward Fisher died at the Kismayo Airport in Somalia, the victim of a terrorist attack. Six months earlier, he sat for an in-depth interview with *Forbes* magazine, the last official interview before his tragic death. The interview, "Edward Fisher: The Comeback King," was published in November 2036.

This was the third *Forbes* interview with Fisher. The first was in 1994, when Fisher, at just 24 years old, first made the *Forbes* "World's Billionaires" list. The second interview was in 2016, by which time he had held the title of the wealthiest person in the world for fifteen years running. The third and final interview took place when Fisher was 66 years old. Below are key excerpts from the last interview.

Forbes: In 2016, we wrote, "For all his seemingly casual demure, Fisher is an incredibly skilled and tenacious business shark. He never lets go of his targeted business prey until he's either devoured them completely or has eaten his fill and discarded the less profitable remains." How do you respond today to this description?

Fisher: That's funny — I've never looked at myself as a business shark. But I've always been competitive, and I know I have confidence in my business decisions. I have my parents to thank for that. And I have my own sense of what's important and how to get the job done. Especially back in my earlier business career,

I remember always pushing myself to make my ideas a reality, and then constantly striving to improve them. I was relentless with myself — I guess others might have interpreted those characteristics as shark-like.

Forbes: Twenty years ago, you were famous for your long-standing reign as the wealthiest man in the world, a title you held for almost two decades. In 2024, you lost that position after donating $240 billion to the Global Earth/Mars Initiative, which you founded that same year. But just twelve years later, in 2036, the success of your Infrastructure Mega-Project Fund had you, once again, among the top ten wealthiest people in the world. How does it feel to be back on top?

Fisher: Come on, when you're worth hundreds of billions of dollars, it doesn't matter — unless you're just plain greedy. This milestone wasn't even on my radar. I mean, if I saw an opportunity present itself where I believed I needed to donate my money to another non-profit enterprise for a good reason, I'd unload this new pile of money in a heartbeat.

Forbes: IMPF, almost from the beginning, was considered the largest fund in the world[1], exceeding BlackRock's $6 trillion in holdings in less than two years. Within the first four years, you amassed an investment war chest of over $13 trillion. In fact, you were so successful in raising capital during the startup phase that the fund quickly had a massive excess of dry powder [uninvested cash on hand]. How did you end up with so much dry powder? Didn't you and your team already have the projects selected?

Fisher: Ah, yes. The dry powder. Well, first, let me say no, we did not have all the projects selected at that time. We sort of knew which hundred or so cities would be involved, but not definitively. Remember, we were (and still are) a commercial vendor, so we had to reach out to each prospective client city and pitch the project, especially in the early years. I mean, we were probably going to lend them the capital at very low-interest rates, and engineer and manage the project, but still, they were going to pay for it.

The simple answer to the dry powder question is it was complicated. Each project took forever to finalize. Design and finance sessions with the principals, the public forums, and on and on. It just took us a while to get all the projects in the pipeline. I guess I was faster at getting investors — the money really started to flow. But some of this money had to sit for a while in low-return accounts. I sure wasn't giving it back to the investors if I could avoid it.

Forbes: What about the criticism from some investors that you were slow to execute projects?

Fisher: It really wasn't that long, in any case. Within three to four years, by 2029 or so, we were pretty much fully engaged. And while we made money from the financial instruments [loans] and each project's engineering and management, we did some good, too. Believe me, the detractors quieted down when they started to see a return on their investments — especially when coupled with the positive environmental impact. We were very careful to quantify before and after relevant environmental variables.

Forbes: Both you and IMPF have been described as altruistic, and economists through the years have used IMPF as a model for what many have called the "new" capitalistic corporate model focusing more on social good and less on just realizing a profit. Is this an accurate picture?

Fisher: Altruistic? Maybe. I *did* hand over $240 billion of my wealth to GEMI. Of course, I initially kept, like, $100 billion in my back pocket, so I'm not sure how altruistic I was. With IMPF, we had three objectives from the beginning. One, make money for our investors. I mean, it's all well and good to invest in socially acceptable projects, but the investors sure as hell still want to make money. Two, select and execute projects in line with our mission: large infrastructure projects designed to dramatically reduce the carbon footprint of the cities involved. And, three, aggressively leverage, in any way possible, the multiplier effect within the locale of each project. I'm as proud of this as I am for all the progress made by IMPF and GEMI over the years. Get this: We're going to realize twenty to fifty times the initial investment in each project, in local economic growth, because of how we manage the cash flowing through these projects. I mean, that's tens of trillions back into these regions.

Forbes: Mr. Fisher, you are alternately praised and vilified for every utterance, every action you take. You can literally move markets with an off-hand comment. Does knowing this affect your behavior in any way?

Fisher: Guys like me are dangerous when we open our mouths! Seriously though, no. Maybe thirty years ago? I don't know — I've been in the spotlight a long time. You get used to it. But I'll put this to you: Humility aside, I can understand why people react to my comments. I have a strong track record of getting things done. Big things. I've been blessed with, I don't know, a doggedness.

Forbes: One last question. Do you have any regrets in your lifetime?

Fisher: You know, not for my past actions. It's water under the bridge anyway, but I think I've done a decent job maneuvering through life so far. But, damn, I wish I had more time and energy to go after the business end of space colonization and exploration. We're already up there, of course, but with GEMI's graphene sheathing and space elevator, SpaceX's space transportation business, and so many others already heading for the stars, it's rich in opportunities that will eventually eclipse Earth's business machine. But, hey, I still have too much work to do in IMPF, and there are just so many hours in a day.

---

[1]"Largest fund in the world" is a slight misrepresentation in that IMPF, while structured as a fund for investors, employed specialty banking instruments for the large, complex financial arrangements

related to the major city projects they undertook worldwide. IMPF was also involved in the engineering and management of each project, ensuring quality work while protecting its investment.

IMPF Dismantles Its Business

2047

Late in the 2020s, Edward Fisher, with urging from Dr. Baptista, devised a plan to refocus global investments to space beginning sometime in the late 2040s. Dr. Baptista had convinced Fisher that towards the middle of the century, we would reach a critical point in the development of a space ecosystem that would demand more investment capital (by a factor of ten) than his predictive analysis suggested would be available. He insisted we needed to shift more capital investments to space-based ventures during this timeframe. Otherwise, he argued, we will risk losing momentum, potentially wasting a generation of valuable human resources, trillions of dollars in invested capital, and related technological advances.

Fisher responded with a plan to dismantle IMPF once 90% of IMPF's originally identified mega-city infrastructure projects around the world had been completed. When this milestone was achieved, IMPF would sell its engineering and construction portfolios to carefully vetted local businesses. IMPF would also create a holding company to administer the hundreds of financial packages by then in place to assist municipalities in financing their infrastructure projects. This, too, would be shut down once these assets were retired or sold. Any profits from these activities would be dispersed to their investors, freeing up trillions of dollars in usable investment capital — hopefully to be reinvested in space ventures.

Fisher's logic was recorded in the minutes of the IMPF board meeting held to ratify this addendum to IMPF bylaws. He explained, "I agree with Dr. Baptista's projections for the investment capital we need to fuel space ecosystem growth towards the middle of the century. And while our mission is important, by that time, it will be more important to give the fledgling space ecosystem every opportunity to grow and flourish. Yes, we will be removing IMPF from the playing field, but we'll work with local engineering and construction companies to ensure they grab the baton and finish what we started. In addition to freeing up the capital necessary for space investments, shifting these projects to local businesses will also further strengthen the economies they operate within."

Not everyone was happy with Fisher's decision to dismantle IMPF. Patrick McDonald, a spokesperson for an IMPF shareholder advocacy group, decried the decision, stating, "Maybe Mr. Fisher feels IMPF should take a bullet for the greater good, but we are talking trillions of dollars in investor capital riding on this act, not his money." Still, Fisher pushed the addendum through, memorializing his endgame for IMPF and his hopes for the future of the nascent space ecosystem.

IMPF grew quickly through the next two decades as the global race to reach net zero carbon emissions heated up, peaking in 2047, with assets of $76 trillion. In the same year, IMPF achieved Fisher's 90% milestone[1], and during its third-quarter 2047 shareholders meeting, then IMPF CEO Patricia Koenigsberg announced, "Per our corporate bylaws, when 90% of our original projects are completed, we are required to shut down the business. Well, here we are. IMPF and its subsidiaries will be sold in the most profitable manner, as quickly as possible, with the profits dispersed to our shareholders." They completed the dissolution in 2052, after selling regional segments of its sprawling global business to eighty-seven carefully vetted, locally owned engineering and infrastructure construction companies; retiring/selling all outstanding financial assets; and reimbursing shareholders.

In a 2052 article covering the final days of IMPF, the *Wall Street Journal* reported that between 2047 and 2052, IMPF shed over $67 trillion in assets. The article further stated, "It is not feasible to quantify how much of Fisher's unprecedented financial gamble resulted in additional space investments during this period. However, during the same timeframe, there was a steady increase in space-related investments of roughly $80 trillion, suggesting as much as $35 trillion might be attributed to IMPF-liberated investment monies. From beyond the grave, Edward Fisher proved his last financial maneuver was a major success."

[1]This milestone had, in fact, been achieved in 2042-3. However, the consequences of this were not recognized until a routine corporate by-laws review in 2045. Subsequent research confirmed the numbers, and CEO Koenigsberg initiated the dissolution of IMPF in 2047.

CLIMATE CHANGE

The 2020s bore witness to an increase in extreme weather around the world, amplifying the growing recognition of the damage humans have done to Earth's biosphere. However, this era also heralded an international acceptance of our collective responsibility for the natural resources critical to the health of Earth — and our willingness to fix what we damaged. While the effects of global warming will remain for some time, we have made prodigious progress in the remedial work needed across our biosphere and in ensuring we remain vigilant stewards of the physical world we call home.

The State of Climate Change in the 2020s

2025

The *State of the World Report* (aka, the *Fisher Report*) was clear regarding the threat of allowing "the world systems to continue status quo." The scientists who authored the report warned that global warming would accelerate without an immediate and concerted world effort and reach a tipping point before the mid twenty-first century. If this dire milestone were reached, they said, there would be no discernible course of action to avert the ensuing catastrophic cascade of environmental changes. These statements were accompanied by irrefutable data collected and analyzed by the several hundred scientists Edward Fisher enlisted to produce the report.

Even before the *Fisher Report* so succinctly stated the urgent warning, governments were attempting to understand the magnitude of the challenge and create a timeline for remediation. The Paris Agreement of 2016 bound almost 200 countries to the goal of dramatically reducing global greenhouse gas (GHG) emissions in an attempt to limit an increase in global warming to no more than 1.5 degrees Celsius above preindustrial levels. In a 2018 report, the Intergovernmental Panel on Climate Change (IPCC) stated unequivocally: "A path exists to 1.5° C, but the window for achieving it is declining rapidly. Furthermore, we must reduce GHG emissions by 45 percent by 2030 and achieve carbon neutrality by 2050."

The global environmental profile of the 2020s was dramatically different from that of the 2050s. Today's governments uniformly adhere to stringent international CO_2 emissions standards. While we have successfully reduced global CO_2 emissions by over 95%, we are still vigilant. The recently published 2054 annual *World Energy Outlook* report from the International Energy Agency (IEA) stated the world is within 4% of obtaining global net zero CO_2 emissions. The report predicts we will reach 98% by 2060 — the statistical equivalent to an ideal 100% CO_2 emissions–free world.

However, in the mid-2020s, there were no legally binding international emissions standards, and almost every major global environmental impact indicator reinforced the grim predictions from most experts. The confluence of environmental abuses through the last several centuries — accelerating after the Industrial Revolution — led to critically elevated air and water pollution; large swaths of deforestation in the most critical forests in the world, reducing by roughly 20% their ability to act as carbon sinks; and ozone layer depletion — all contributing to global warming and subsequent disruptive climate changes. In 2019, the Intergovernmental Science-Policy Platform on Biodiversity and Ecosystem Services (IPBES) published the *Global Assessment Report on Biodiversity and Ecosystem Services*. The IPBES Chair at the time, Sir Robert Watson, warned in the report, "The overwhelming evidence of the IPBES Global Assessment, from a wide range of different fields of knowledge, presents an ominous picture. ..." He continued, "The health of ecosystems upon which we and all other species depend is deteriorating more rapidly than ever. We are eroding the very foundations of our economies, livelihoods, food security, health, and quality of life worldwide."

The 2020s was the decade when government and business leaders throughout the world began, albeit initially in a haphazard fashion, to mend the environment they had nearly destroyed. Through large international initiatives, the efforts became more focused, fueling a global movement in the decades leading up to the 2050s. Such initiatives included the early Kyoto Protocol, the Paris Agreement, and the United Nations Framework Convention on Climate Change (UNFCCC); the unprecedented World Biosphere Protection Treaty of 2027 (WBPT); organized international grassroots groups such as the mega-cities C40 collaborative, the Global Covenant of Mayors for Climate and Energy (GCoM) and the Davos Conference; and the ambitious, multifaceted Global Earth/Mars Initiative (GEMI) and Infrastructure Mega-Project Fund (IMPF).

Banding Together against Global Warming

2029

Since the early twenty-first century, most scientists and business and government leaders recognized the time-sensitive need to reduce CO_2 emissions worldwide. However, with notable exceptions such as Morocco, Costa Rica, The Gambia, and India, the aggressive reduction of CO_2 emissions was not a demonstrable priority for most countries, especially in their larger, complex urban centers. Unlike the 2050s, when approximately 94% of our world's urban centers are now certified carbon-neutral, in 2025, the idea of a carbon-neutral city was still a lofty and expensive goal. While several smaller cities were boasting a carbon-neutral footprint, all were making heavy use of carbon offsets to push their net CO_2 emissions down to zero.

Regardless, mayors in hundreds of small and large municipalities recognized that with 60% of the world's population living in urban areas in the mid-2020s, *true* carbon-neutral city planning and development were crucial to meeting this goal – and were within their purview to remediate. Leveraging regional governments, the World Biosphere Protection Treaty (WBPT), IMPF, and other sources for financing and expertise, city mayors banded together with large alliances such as C40, the Health and Environment Alliance (HEAL), Global Earth/Mars Initiative (GEMI), Climate Alliance, and hundreds of smaller grassroots groups to tackle global warming at local and regional levels.

Concurrent with their local efforts, these cities, together with prominent NGOs and university systems with tens of trillions of dollars in pension and employee retirement funds, began to pressure financial giants like BlackRock and JPMorgan Chase to shift their investment portfolios to align with environmental, social, and corporate governance (ESG) sustainability ideals. Commonly referred to as sustainable, responsible, and impact investing (SRI) tools, these funds primarily focused on generating acceptable returns for investors and positively impacting societal changes. This sustained pressure was profoundly successful. Statista (a leading provider of market and consumer data) reported that in 2055, mainstream investment funds worldwide totaled about $740 trillion US. These included pensions, mutual and hedge funds, sovereign wealth funds (SWF), and private equity, with 87% of these funds (approximately $590 trillion) defined as SRI funds.

These efforts proved key in helping to turn the tide and realize an essentially carbon-neutral global society by 2055. This sustained, concerted campaign succeeded because of the decades-long efforts of the leadership within cities, NGOs, university systems, and later, governments around the world. In a show of extraordinary collaboration and will, they leveraged their enormous collective expertise, wealth, and capacity to meet the CO_2 emissions reduction goals.

By the early 2030s, GEMI had developed a close partnership with the C40 leadership and organization, as well as member cities near GEMI centers. They began to work together to model and template the processes involved in CO_2 reduction action plans. Dr. Duarte described the rationale for creating the partnership.

"The C40 group had a well-thought-out plan of action with a smart timeline and practical, attainable goals. By that time, C40 had over a hundred member cities in as many countries, all committed to bringing their cities down to a net-zero CO_2 emissions status," she said. "This consortium of mega-cities alone accounts for almost 25% of the world's GDP and is home to one in twelve people worldwide. We welcomed the opportunity to partner with this powerful and organized network of motivated cities."

Author's note: *As a precursor to GEMI's 2028 formal statement against the long-term use of carbon credits, Dr. Duarte required all GEMI centers to be carbon-neutral from the day they opened. Still, during the development phase for each center, even GEMI utilized carbon offsets to realize a carbon-neutral footprint. As each center became fully operational and carbon-neutral systems were implemented, carbon offsets were decreased in equal quantities — eventually yielding a truly carbon-neutral footprint.*

World Biosphere Protection Treaty

2027

In her opening remarks, U.N. Secretary-General Dr. Jill Mandela set the tone for the 2027 U.N. Climate Change Conference, COP32, as such: "We are at war, but we still have a clear path to victory. Will we take that path, as difficult as it may be? Or, will we continue to arrogantly stay on our current course, nearly certain that the destination, although of our choosing, will not be to our liking? I say we take the path to victory." The COP32 delegates agreed.

The World Biosphere Protection Treaty (WBPT) ratification in 2027 at COP32 was a seminal event in the decades-long battle against global warming. Indeed, never before have the countries of the world come together so completely to stave off a common foe. This grand, ambitious international treaty created pools of capital, technology, and human resources to restore, grow, and protect the hundreds of forests, wetlands, and ocean habitats around the world deemed essential to the survival of humanity — regardless of their locations. WBPT shifted the primary responsibility for protecting these vital resources from individual sovereign countries to the international community of countries.

Built on the previously instituted, reactive "loss and damage" fund[1], WBPT was a proactive program modeled after existing intra-country payments for environmental services (PES)[2] programs and the best features of hundreds of existing transboundary protected areas (TBPA)[3].

Each participating country's annual financial contribution to WBPT was tied to its quantified CO_2 emissions output for the prior year. At the time, CO_2 emissions correlated closely with a country's GDP, so the wealthiest developed countries in the world carried the brunt of the WBPT funding, while the remainder was levied on global financial, energy, and pharmaceutical conglomerates[4]. The World Bank, in its 2052 special report, *WBPT at Twenty-Five*, stated that from the inception of WBPT through 2052, countries of the world contributed over $33 trillion[5] to the treaty, while corporate "contributions" accounted for $22 trillion (adjusted to 2050 dollars).

The guidance, technology, and recurring PESs supplied by WBPT enabled countries to restore vital resources and biodiversity while assisting local communities in building sustainable futures. Indeed, the roughly 800 million people living near these resources worldwide depended on these natural resources for their livelihoods, shelter, food, water, and energy security. The PESs were variable and tied to key performance indicators (KPIs) that described the state of the local biosystems based on data collected and analyzed, piecemeal at first, then, beginning in 2031, by the satellite-based Global Environmental Monitoring System (GEMS)[6].

GEMS, launched in 2031, is still considered the standard for accurately measuring the multitude of pollutants and other contributing factors involved in global warming and ecosystem degradation. This capacity to accurately measure physical and chemical environmental changes anywhere in the world in near real-time was critical to WBPT. As GEMS-monitored local ecosystems recovered and communities transitioned to economies in harmony with their environments, PESs were decreased just enough to maintain stasis, relieving some of the financial burdens of the contributing countries and corporations.

Other systems were also developed to aid communities in optimizing their local businesses' trade of consumables, products, and services to compete in existing and emerging local, regional, and global markets. These comprehensive business systems — which factored in weather, crop yields, supply chains, neighboring communities, other competitive pressures, and PES payments — provided the necessary data, business intelligence, and commercial outlets for these communities to thrive in today's world.

WBPT has had enduring, inestimable positive effects on Earth's biosphere and the world economy. This far-reaching collaboration played a central role in the global battle to halt and reverse decades of high CO_2 emissions and biosphere degradation worldwide. Tens of trillions of dollars were invested in this effort, enabling millions of families, small businesses, and communities to reinvent themselves, helping the world to ensure a new level of environmental security for the future. Midway through the 2050s, WBPT still stands as a bulwark against human endangerment of the Earth's biosphere ever again.

———————————

[1] In 2022, delegates at the 27th annual United Nations Climate Change Conference (COP27) voted nearly unanimously to "… establish and operationalize a fund to compensate vulnerable nations for 'loss and damage' from climate-induced disasters."

[2] Payments for environmental services (also known as payments for ecosystem services or PES) are payments to farmers or landowners who have agreed to take certain actions to manage their land or watersheds to provide an ecological service.

[3] An ecologically protected area that spans the boundaries of more than one country or sub-national entity (Wikipedia, 2028).

[4] Citing corporate historic responsibilities for contributing to global warming and extreme weather, WBPT (with proxy authority through the world leadership) levied annual international taxes on these industries. This amounted to hundreds of billions of dollars each year to help pay for WBPT programs around the world.

[5] This includes $4.6 trillion dispersed through the loss and damages fund and $1.3 trillion spent by the countries receiving the payment for environmental services (PES), per WBPT self-investment requirements.

[6] The Global Environmental Monitoring System, developed and maintained pro bono by GEMI, is a satellite-based biosphere monitor-

ing system. It is unrivaled in its accuracy and is utilized by thousands of entities worldwide for various climate-related measurements.

Global Environmental Monitoring System (GEMS)

2031

In 2027, COP32 delegates ratified the World Biosphere Protection Treaty (WBPT)[1]. The key treaty component, the PES programs, demanded accurate environmental measurements. However, systems available to monitor the multitude of pollutants and other contributing indicators involved in global warming and ecosystem degradation were inadequate. The United Nations Framework Convention on Climate Change (UNFCCC) decided they needed to develop a next-generation global environmental monitoring system (GEMS) to address this need.

Launched in 2031, GEMS included hundreds of satellites strategically placed to blanket the Earth. This dense array of satellites allowed GEMS to collect data on hundreds of physical and chemical elements across Earth's entire geosphere, biosphere, cryosphere, hydrosphere, and atmosphere. The loci of most of these measures were identifiable to within less than one kilometer anywhere on the surface of Earth.

As innovative as the satellite system was, the software was the heart of GEMS. Working closely with the UNFCCC Subsidiary Body for Scientific and Technological Advice (SBSTA), GEMI volunteered to develop the complex monitoring, descriptive, and predictive reporting system at no cost to the international community. Dr. Hana Duarte explained GEMI's generosity with a shrug.

"We were just doing our part as members of the global community," she said. "The WBPT was an amazing breakthrough in the collective fight to restore and protect our global ecosystems — and perfectly aligned with our GEMI mission. GEMS has comprehensive, granular, quantitative feedback critical to the timely disbursements of the WBPT's PES funds to thousands of communities worldwide. It was a privilege to develop GEMS and commit to maintain and upgrade the system for free."

In an interview with *Information Week* in March 2035, Dr. Patrick Farley, chief scientist for Computational Systems Biology at Oak Ridge National Laboratory and the Cray/MIT supercomputer collaboration project leader, described the unprecedented volume of data continuously streaming into the system. "Our CrayX is one of the fastest supercomputers in the world, but we're still adding nodes every few weeks to keep up with the computational needs of GEMS. And the storage needed for the data collected by the system is astronomical," he said. "It's crazy to contemplate, but the GEMS database grew by a little over one zettabyte this past year [2034] alone. Even though the CrayX was made for this type of demand, we're just able to keep up."

The UNFCCC created a separate organization to manage and operate the massive GEMS. This organization included specialists from nearly every country on Earth — including many GEMI alums who were involved in the initial development of GEMS. In addition to conducting WBPT-related data collection and reporting, these scientists and technicians used this mountain of data to refine evolving climate models, detect environmental smoking guns, and track and proactively plot the next steps to remediate their local environs. Dashboards were also made available to each country's leadership detailing the near real-time metrics within their borders.

By the late-2030s, GEMS' precision measurements had become the universally accepted source for hundreds of critical indices related to global warming. Indeed, communities, governments, and corporations worldwide still utilize GEMS data to create environmental profiles and benchmarks, quantify the environmental impact of construction projects, and certify their CO_2 footprints to garner available carbon credits and government incentives.

-----

[1]In 2027, the United Nations Framework Convention on Climate Change (UNFCCC) ratified a global treaty to protect the natural resources necessary to sustain a healthy world ecosystem.

Last Fossil-fuel Powered Car Manufactured

2039

From the invention of the commercially viable internal combustion engine (ICE) in the late 1800s to the year 2027, fossil fuel–propelled vehicles were the dominant mode of transportation for land and air travel throughout the world. While electric vehicles (EVs) have been in existence for at least as long as ICE-based vehicles, they were considered a novelty and did not enter the mainstream until automotive giant Toyota released the hybrid[1] Prius in 2000. Jato Dynamics, an automobile intelligence company, reported in a 2019 article that internal combustion engines (i.e., fossil fuel sources) counted for over 90% of global car sales in the first half of 2019. In 2020, more than 1.4 billion automobiles were operating worldwide, and 94% of them had an ICE. In contrast, the 2053 *World Transportation Report* stated, "Globally, this past year [2052], 98% of all passenger vehicles were fossil fuel–free."

The transition to a fossil fuel–free transportation model was a challenge for most countries to implement. The *New York Times*, in an April 2021 article describing auto industry trends, discussed how this transition might occur in America: "If the United States wanted to move to a fully electric fleet by 2050 — to meet President Biden's goal of net-zero emissions — then sales of gasoline-powered vehicles would likely have to end altogether by around 2035, a heavy lift."

The authors then postulate on contributing factors to the decline of ICE-powered vehicles: "One possibility is that the nation reaches a tipping point: As more and more plug-in vehicles start appearing on the roads, gas stations and crude oil refineries start closing down, while auto repair shops shift to mainly servicing electric models. Eventually, it might be too much of a hassle for people to own conventional gasoline-powered cars."

Although it would take a few years longer to realize, this is precisely what occurred. EV sales continued to accelerate through the 2020s. By 2030, fully 76% of all vehicles sold worldwide were EVs. By this time, charging stations for EVs commanded 65% of the refueling real estate versus 35% for traditional gas stations for fossil fuel–propelled vehicles. Many factors contributed to the acceleration of EV sales and the corresponding decline of ICE-powered vehicle ownership. Governments around the world offered incentives to purchase EVs and trade-in ICE vehicles. Many countries also significantly increased fossil fuel taxes, further disincentivizing the ownership of ICE-powered vehicles.

Arguably the primary technological disruptor in the shift to EV-based transportation was the solar energy collecting "skin" developed by GEMI researchers in the early 2030s. Covering approximately half of a vehicle's external surface, this dense micro-filament mesh was baked into the shell of the vehicle, collecting energy from the sun and continuously recharging the vehicle's batteries. On average, this skin tripled the distance an EV could travel on one battery charge. By 2040, this breakthrough technology was a standard feature on over 60% of new EVs. The International Energy Agency (IEA), in their 2050 *Global Energy Report*, stated, "GEMI's surface-embedded solar energy collector technology alone was responsible for reducing transportation-based CO_2 emissions by 9% over the last ten years."

Further, by the early 2030s, most automobile companies had all but abandoned the development of new or improved ICE-based models, focusing almost entirely on the still-accelerating EV market. As the range and quality of EV offerings within the car and light truck categories grew, the production of remaining ICE models dwindled. Around the world, consumers embraced EVs, leaving the small but niche ICE vehicle industry to fade until government mandates in major global markets shut it down in the late 2030s.

China's Xieng Corporation produced the last ICE-powered vehicle in 2038. More like a four-wheeled motorcycle than a conventional car, the Xio was a two-seat vehicle with a simple four-cycle engine. While rivaling similarly sized EVs with its 337-mpg rating, there was no real market for the Xio, and Xieng discontinued the model. It is estimated that as many as half of the Xios manufactured in 2038 were immediately sequestered as collector's items.

After 2038, all new vehicles sold in the car, light and heavy truck, and motorcycle categories worldwide were zero-emissions vehicles.

––––––––––

[1]Hybrid electric vehicles are powered by an internal combustion engine and one or more electric motors, which use energy stored in batteries. A hybrid electric vehicle cannot be plugged in to charge the battery. Instead, the battery is charged through regenerative braking and by the internal combustion engine (U.S. Department of Energy, 2026).

Thirty Years of Global Power Generation

2025 — 2055

One of the biggest obstacles to global decarbonization was supplying low-carbon emission energy to the world's existing and emerging markets. This goal was complex, crossing technologies, borders, industries, and energy sectors. Over nearly two centuries since the Industrial Revolution, most industries developed technologies using fossil-based fuels, either directly or indirectly, in the latter case generating electricity via fossil fuel–powered power plants. Converting to renewable energy sources would take trillions of dollars in new investments and trillions more potentially lost in abandoning existing fossil fuel–based systems. Still, the endgame was worth the effort — the potential for low-carbon electrification of the world.

There are three types of fossil fuel–based energy: coal, oil, and natural gas. Likewise, there are three types of renewable low-carbon energy: wind, solar, and hydroelectric — plus nuclear power. In a 2020 *Our World in Data* article, "Electricity," Hannah Ritchie wrote, "In 2019, almost two-thirds (63.3%) of global electricity came from fossil fuels. Of the 36.7% from low-carbon sources, renewables accounted for 26.3% and nuclear energy for 10.4%." By this time, most world leaders recognized the need to reduce human-generated carbon dioxide emissions to net zero by mid-century, and in 2016 nearly 200 nations ratified the Paris Agreement framework for climate change. Governments slowly began to shift to low-carbon energy sources by refurbishing and adding new nuclear plants, and by aggressively adopting and expanding renewable wind, solar, and hydroelectric energy solutions to meet the growing global power demand.

The International Energy Agency (IEA) 2020 Energy Technology Perspective predicted how these efforts might unfold for the future of renewables in global power generation. The report stated, "Solar photovoltaics (PV), wind and other modern renewable energy technologies, together with nuclear power and fossil fuel power plants equipped with CCUS, convert energy into electricity without emitting significant amounts of CO_2, while the rapid growth of electrification extends low-carbon power to more end uses. The share of renewables (including bioenergy with carbon capture, utilization, and storage [CCUS], or bioenergy with carbon capture and storage [BECCS]) in the global power generation mix reaches 86% in 2070, with the remaining 14% of power [coming] from nuclear plants (8%), fossil fuel plants with CCUS (5%) and hydrogen (1%)."

The IEA was correct that there would be a significant shift to global power generation from renewables. However, these shifts came sooner than most experts anticipated. In an updated Energy Technology Perspective for 2055, the IEA stated, "By 2055, the share of renewables within the global power generation mix was 83%, with solar and wind accounting for 68%, and CCUS, BECCS and hydro the remaining 15%. The share of renewables in the global power generation mix will reach 92% by 2070."

Power companies and governments continued through the 2030s to retire aging nuclear-powered energy plants, shutting down more than 120 of them between 2020 and 2050. Still, nuclear power plants nearly tripled to 1,203 worldwide during the same timeframe. Most new nuclear plants developed in the 2030s and 2040s have been smaller, pebble-based reactors with few moving parts. These reactors are about a third more efficient than older reactor models; they are also safer and more reliable, with minimal negative impact resulting from an accident.

Solar-generated energy installations continued to grow at accelerated rates through the mid-2030s. However, this growth slowed to 4-5% per year through the 2040s. The International Solar Energy Society (ISES)'s 2037 article, "The Future of Solar Energy," stated, "While solar energy capacity should continue to grow at a rate of 4-5% annually until at least 2050, gone is the double-digit annual growth of the last fifteen years." Still, in 2050, solar power capacity reached 10,881 GW, or 36% of the installed electrical capacity worldwide, becoming the largest renewable energy source.

Wind-generated energy capacity also grew dramatically through the 2020s, primarily onshore, as smaller wind farm models built within local and regional locations worldwide became the norm. However, according to Statista, by 2036, offshore wind farms' energy capacity (1,704 GW) overtook onshore wind farm capacity (1,490 GW). This was primarily due to the increased size and efficiencies of the offshore farms. Also, as new, higher-capacity energy-transportation infrastructures were built, offshore wind farms became economically competitive with onshore wind-generated energy. By 2055, the IEA reported that total wind-generated power reached 9,613 GW, fully 32% of total electricity capacity worldwide.

Growth in global hydroelectricity capacity began to slow in the late 2020s but stabilized through the 2030s and 2040s, maintaining an average of nearly 3% annual growth for that period. In 2055, hydropower generation accounted for 9% (2,717 GW) of electrical power capability worldwide.

Worldwide installed electrical capacity reached nearly 32,000 GW in 2055 (IEA Energy Technology Perspective for 2055). Across all energy generation sectors, a reduction in project sizes drove the propagation of renewable electricity technologies. Smaller, more manageable projects lessened the demand for long-haul power transportation and reduced the risk of power grid–related terrorist attacks.

The World's Forests Recover

2025 — 2055

In the mid-2020s, forests accounted for approximately four billion hectares or 31% of the world's land surface. This equated to a loss of nearly 50% of the world's forests in the last 10,000 years, with half of this loss occurring since 1900. The many causes of this dangerous, systemic deforestation included mining, the increased need for agriculture and livestock ranching (especially cattle), logging, overpopulation, and climate change. Although it was virtually impossible to attempt to recoup the entire four billion hectares, many scientists believe that even with humanity's extensive global footprint, there is the potential to reclaim as much as ten percent of the world's lost forests. Dr. Zhang Che, a researcher at Northeast Forestry University (NEFU), China, wrote in a *Nature* journal article in 2035, "Our model details how Earth can sustain upwards of one-half billion additional hectares of forests worldwide, without undue hardships to our collective way of life."

While there were thousands of active reforestation and afforestation projects worldwide during this time, most of the larger, successful efforts have been attributed to the World Biosphere Protection Treaty (WBPT), ratified in 2027. This unprecedented international agreement shifted the financial responsibility for protecting the natural resources identified as essential to the health of Earth to the international community of nations. The historic accord secured the funding needed to restore and protect these essential resources and aid the thousands of local communities depending on them for their livelihoods. Indeed, Dr. Lydia Pernia, in her first speech as director of the newly founded WBPT, cautioned, "The socioeconomic environments local to these global treasures are the primary drivers of the success or failure of these grand conservation initiatives. If we do not assist these local communities in finding a way forward in harmony with our biosphere, our efforts will probably utterly fail within the decade."

In 2030, WBPT began distributing monies and other resources to thousands of targeted reforestation and afforestation projects world-wide — some with prodigious results. One such project was the development of the Great Green Wall in northern Africa. Started in 2007 and led by the African Union, the project involved the collaboration of twenty nations to plant millions of trees to combat desertification as the Sahara Desert expanded along eleven of their contiguous northern borders. The African Union declared the Great Green Wall completed in 2038, thirty-one years after the project began, at a cost of $42 billion — $26 billion of which was from WBPT-sponsored programs. This 4,000-mile-long, miles-wide band of forest spans the Sahel region of the northern African continent, from Djibouti on the eastern coast to Senegal on the western coast, its unique green band strikingly visible from space.

Another successful program was the aggressive, strategic afforestation of vast tracks of barren and unusable lands in western China. The Chinese government initiated the Conversion of Cropland to Forest Program (CCFP)[1] "payments for environmental services" (PES) program in 1999 in response to repeated catastrophic flooding in its extensive western farmlands. Dubbed "Grain for Green," the program paid farmers to plant trees on their land and provided degraded land to rural families to restore. By the time WBPT was ratified in the late 2020s, roughly 40 million hectares of secondary forest[2] had already been regained.

The WBPT architects recognized this success and incorporated much of the decades long CCFP PES program in the plan's framework.

Many groups — GEMI among them — trekked to China to learn firsthand from leaders of these programs. Together with WBPT funding, CCFP-like programs continued to reclaim forest lands. According to the China Forestry Economics and Development Research Center (FEDRC) 2050 Annual Report, 79 million hectares of secondary forest cover have been reclaimed or realized since the inception of CCFP.

Tropical primary forests[3] and secondary forests are resilient and opportunistic in their quest to regenerate. The Amazon, for example, is the largest tropical rainforest on Earth, encompassing nine countries in its embrace and claiming 52% of the world's primary forests. Still, by the end of the 2020s, the Amazon, in less than one hundred years, had lost an alarming 95 million hectares of forest cover due to unchecked deforestation. In 2030, fueled by WBPT funding and support, eight of the nine countries owning portions of the Amazon began the largest tropical forest reforestation effort in history.

A short twenty-five years later, GEMS[4] reported this immense reforestation project had reclaimed over 70 million hectares of forest, approximately 65% of which is in the razed portions of eastern Brazil. In his third-term inaugural speech in 2054, Brazilian President Luiz Godói praised world leaders and the WBPT, stating, "The global community, in implementing the World Biosphere Protection Treaty, have all but assured the vast 'a Amazônia', as well as other forest systems of the world, will flourish into the future. For this, we Brazilians, for our country and as global citizens, are grateful."

The dramatic deforestation slowdown witnessed in the 2030s and 2040s, coupled with the aggressive early WBPT reforestation and afforestation programs, yielded extraordinary outcomes. In 2055, GEMS reported that forest coverage worldwide had increased to 36% — adding 200 million hectares, or roughly the size of Mexico. Dr. Theodore Kerr, head of the UN-Biosphere Research Institute, weighed in, "We are really at 36% now — an astounding number that was not even on our radar. Will this growth continue or plateau? Of course, the land available is finite. Our simulations predict a deceleration in the growth of new forest coverage and a plateau of 39% by 2080. But still, these numbers are amazing. We should all be proud of what we have accomplished in bringing the world's forests back to life."

Author's note: GEMI, an unaffiliated international organization with deep pockets, was, by design, heavily involved in the afforestation and reforestation efforts from the organization's founding. However, GEMI declined to contribute money to the WBPT PES programs. When asked why, Dr. Hana Duarte explained, "Yes, GEMI was criticized for not implementing some type of payment for environmental services ourselves. But we didn't think it would be the best use of our money, so we went the fieldwork route instead."

---

[1] Also known as "Grain-for-Green" or the "Sloping Land Conversion Program," the Conversion of Cropland to Forest Program (CCFP) was, for most of the 2020s, the world's largest afforestation-based payments for environmental services (PES) program. It involved over 32 million rural households and an investment of more than $42 billion (until 2013) and has over 27 million hectares of land enrolled (Bennett, Michael T. et al., "China's Conversion of Cropland to Forest Program for Household Delivery of Ecosystem Services: How Important is a Local Implementation Regime to Survival Rate Outcomes?" (September 2014).

[2] A secondary forest (or second-growth forest) is a forest or woodland area which has regenerated through largely natural processes after human-caused disturbances, such as timber harvest or agriculture clearing, or equivalently disruptive natural phenomena (Wikipedia contributors, "Secondary Forest," The Free Encyclopedia, 2033).

[3] A primary forest is a naturally regenerated forest of native tree species where there are no clearly visible indications of human activity, and the ecological processes are not significantly disturbed (The Food and Agriculture Organization of the United Nations, 2036).

[4] UN administered satellite-based monitoring and reporting system capable of identifying thousands of pollutants anywhere on Earth (United Nations, 2039).

The World Ocean

2025 - 2055

The World Ocean comprises five regions — the Pacific, Atlantic, Indian, Arctic, and Southern Oceans — defined by the continents, basins, and other unique geographic features. The World Ocean covers 71% of the Earth's surface (the world's continents fit easily into the Pacific Ocean basin[1] alone) and holds 97% of its water. The ocean is responsible for 50% of the oxygen we breathe and is the largest carbon sink, absorbing roughly 30% of the CO_2 released into the atmosphere and acting as a heat sink for 90% of the excess heat from the Earth's atmosphere. In short, the World Ocean is our lungs and air conditioner. The United Nations, in its 2055 *World Water Development Report*, stated, "More than 3.5 billion people rely on marine and coastal biodiversity for their livelihood." Clearly, our world depends on the World Ocean.

Nevertheless, until recently, humans have flagrantly abused the ocean and its rich and critical ecosystems. For millennia, we dumped refuse, sewage, and more recently, plastics and chemicals into its estuaries and directly into the ocean. Systemic abuse of other global biosystems, combined with chronic overfishing, degraded ocean ecosystems and threatened the economic, housing, and food security of billions of people. Human-generated CO_2 in Earth's atmosphere contributed to global warming, causing the melting of glaciers and other ice formations and a corresponding rise in sea levels. This excess atmospheric CO_2, absorbed by the ocean, resulted in ocean acidification, threatening the myriad wetlands, mangroves, and coral reefs deemed essential to a healthy global biosphere and potentially depriving thousands of species of their natural habitats along the world's coastline and continental shelves[2].

While there have been numerous international attempts to protect the ocean through the centuries, it was ultimately the High Seas[3] Treaty (HST), ratified in 2023 (and amended four times since), that finally established the legal framework to manage and enforce efforts to protect the vast, open ocean. In 2031, the HST was incorporated into the broader World Biosphere Protection Treaty (WBPT), and as with key forest systems around the globe, WBPT has driven many of the advances in our conservation of the ocean during the past nearly twenty-five years. WBPT has also supplied consulting, training, and financial assistance to thousands of coastal communities around the world, helping them adjust to the economic and societal changes necessitated by the international community's remedial environmental solutions.

Nearly 140 sovereign countries with ocean coastlines have internationally recognized jurisdiction over 130 million square kilometers (50 million square miles) of territorial seas[4] and exclusive economic zones (EEZs)[5]. Most of this ocean property lies within broad continental shelves covered by relatively shallow water averaging about 60 meters (200 feet) in depth. By 2032, world leaders were leveraging WBPT funding and expertise, developing Marine Protected Areas (MPAs)[6], Marine Protected Area Networks (MPANs) [7], and Other Effective area-based Conservation Measures (OECMs) [8] across these zones and the High Seas. According to WBPT statistics, by 2050, these protected areas accounted for 47% of the territorial and national EEZ zones and 72% of the international High Seas, bringing the total protected area to approximately 206 million square kilometers (80 million square miles) — or nearly two-thirds of the entire ocean.

One early WBPT project was the rehabilitation of the Pasig River in the Philippines. The Pasig River is only 25 kilometers (15.5 miles) in length, spanning the main island of Luzon, but was considered among the biggest chemical and plastics river polluters of the ocean. GEMI, one of the earlier organizations tackling ocean plastics pollution, had purposefully placed one of its centers near the Pasig, on the outskirts of Manila to assist with the cleanup of the river. In an interview conducted several years after GEMI's efforts had begun to take hold, Dr. Jacob Baptista reflected on the organization's involvement in the project.

"We knew most ocean plastics pollution flows from rivers, and the Pasig was one of the worst offenders. WBPT worked closely with us [GEMI], SMC [San Miguel Corporation], IMPF [Infrastructure Mega-Project Fund], and the Philippine government to stop the pollution and return the river to good health. By the time we arrived on the scene, SMC was already dredging the river," Dr. Baptista said. "I believe they completed the work in 2029 or 2030. We focused on the plastics interception[9] and cleanup, while IMPF partnered with WBPT and the Philippine government to fund and build waste management infrastructures along the entire heavily populated river. The WBPT also worked with the Philippine government to relocate tens of thousands of families away from its banks and tributaries. Today, the river is a real gem."

By 2025, there were an estimated 200 million tons of plastics garbage in the ocean, with an additional 5 million to 20 million tons added yearly — predominantly trillions of pieces of microplastics[10], abandoned commercial fishing nets, and other gear. Still, in large part because of the focus and tenacity of numerous international nonprofit organizations (NPOs) and plastics cleanup companies, efforts to clean up the ocean's surface plastics wastes have been largely successful. The general decline in the production and consumption of single-use plastics products, better international management of plastics waste and recycling, and the river-based interception of floating plastics worldwide certainly helped. By the late 2040s, these cumulative efforts had essentially completed the surface plastics cleanup of the World Ocean.

The development of ocean-based community habitats — once scattered, haphazard, and unregulated — became a commercially viable industry as rising sea levels began threatening the homes and businesses of coastal communities, forcing alternative solutions. Typically, these "floating cities" are relatively inexpensive, carbon-neutral clusters of low-profile platforms. They are usually loosely tethered in shallow water, allowing inhabitants to safely live and work on the ocean (and inland bodies of fresh water) indefinitely. Once GEMI introduced its self-sustaining, low-cost modular Aquapod in 2032, the development of ocean-based floating cities began to accelerate.

Like the Ford Model T of the previous century, the GEMI Aquapod was produced and priced for the masses worldwide. While numerous competitors would enter this market — most notably LilyPod and OceanHabitats — GEMI's market share still exceeds 60% in 2055, according to *Forbes* magazine. GEMI CEO Dr. Hana Duarte noted, "Because of the rising sea level, this type of ocean habitat was desperately needed around the world. I'm happy we were able to supply our Aquapod habitat solution. Also, the profits make up a large portion of our yearly dividends to our member countries. It's a win-win!"

Indeed, IMF stated in its 2055 *Global Habitats* report that there are currently upwards of 160 million people living in floating ocean-based communities globally, with a projected 420 million calling a floating city home by 2065. For example, the citizens of Kiribati[11], an archipelago state in the Pacific Ocean comprising thirty-three small atolls (of which twenty are habitable), were once doomed to watch their island nation slowly disappear as the sea level rose. However, they began assembling floating communities in the late 2020s and are now home to one of the largest per-capita concentrations of floating communities in the world. The 2050 Kiribati Census reported 94% of their citizens now live in floating communities on the ocean. Of these communities, 65% are clustered throughout the broad reef and large lagoon of the Tarawa Atoll, where the floating capital is also located. Kiribati President Martin Timon acknowledged, "Because of global warming and rising sea levels, we did not have much of a choice in embracing floating cities. We had to either abandon our home country or adapt. We adapted, and our people are confident in our sustainable solutions to rising sea levels."

Similar in concept to land-based agriculture, marine aquaculture[12] is the full-cycle farming of shellfish, algae, and other nutrient-rich plants. When designed and managed properly, aquaculture farming requires few inputs and is a sustainable, ecologically friendly source of high-quality, nutritious foods. Technological innovations have led to a dramatic increase in the number, efficiency, and capacity of ocean-based seafood and vegetation farms within national and international waters. Much of this expansion has come from the evolution of satellite monitoring and control systems, versatile robotic submarines, and drones, enabling farmers to practice safer high-volume, cost-effective, sustainable aquaculture. These tools have been especially instrumental in the inherently dangerous High Seas, and the thousands of farms that now dot the High Seas are a testament to the fortitude of such technology.

The Food and Agriculture Organization of the United Nations reported in its 2055 edition of *The State of World Fisheries and Aquaculture* that global seafood production (both capture and aquaculture) was 670 million metric tons, generated $3.7 trillion in revenue, and directly employed more than 100 million people around the world. The report also stated marine aquaculture accounted for 89% of seafood and algae farming production worldwide, with an estimated 72% grown and harvested within territorial and EEZ zones and 28% on the High Seas.

Worldwide, by 2030, fossil fuel generation and consumption began to yield to renewable energy sources. In addition to land-based renewable energy initiatives, governments and power companies began focusing on harvesting offshore wind, solar, and wave energy within national territorial and EEZ zones. Over the next decade, as collection and delivery technologies improved, these offshore renewable solutions surged ahead of land-based energy generation. By 2042, the International Energy Agency (IEA) annual *Energy Technology Perspective* reported, "In 2041, for the first time, the energy generated by ocean-based renewable energy sources exceeded that of land-based sources." This trend has continued, and in 2055, the IEA reported offshore renewable energy accounted for 63% of terrestrial energy generated, with

32% from land-based sources and the remaining 5% from space-based solar energy collection[13].

Midway through the 2050s, MPA networks now protect 59% of the ocean. Tens of millions of people live in floating communities within national territorial waters. We have cleaned up most of the hundreds of millions of pounds of floating garbage we have dumped into the ocean — and we have safeguarded against allowing this mass pollution to occur in the future. We have learned how to harvest enormous amounts of food and energy from the ocean without negatively impacting its ecosystems, all while feeding billions of people and powering more than half the world with clean, renewable energy. Coastal communities around the world, with WBPT assistance, have realigned themselves, helping to ensure their future physical, economic, and food security. This expanded reliance on the ocean is evident around the world as coastal skylines illuminate a patchwork of ocean-based communities, aquaculture farms, and energy collection platforms.

Clearly, we depend more on the ocean now for our survival than we ever have. However, as we close in on 2060, we are also acutely aware of the critical need to pursue and maintain a symbiotic relationship with our World Ocean, rather than perpetuate the parasitic one we have clung to for so long.

---

[1]Covering approximately 63 million square miles, the Pacific Ocean is the largest of the world ocean basins — blanketing roughly one-third of the surface of Earth.

[2]Portions of continents that are submerged under an area of relatively shallow water, known as a sea shelf (Wikipedia, 2033).

[3]The portions of the ocean not within the jurisdiction of any country.

[4]The area defined by the UN Convention on the Law of the Seas as 12 nautical miles, or 22 kilometers, away from a coastal baseline point.

[5]An area of the ocean, generally extending 200 nautical miles (230 miles) beyond a nation's territorial sea, within which a coastal nation

has jurisdiction over both living and nonliving resources (NOAA Ocean Exploration, 2040).

[6]An area of a sea, ocean, estuary, or major lake that restricts human activity for conservation purposes, typically to protect natural or cultural resources. These marine areas exist in many forms, ranging from wildlife refuges to research facilities (Wikipedia, 2033).

[7]A collection of individual MPAs or reserves operating cooperatively and synergistically, at various spatial scales, and with a range of protection levels that are designed to meet objectives that a single reserve cannot achieve (Wikipedia, 2033).

[8]A geographically defined area other than a Marine Protected Area that is governed and managed in ways that achieve positive and sustained long-term outcomes for in-situ conservation of biodiversity. OECMs encompass associated ecosystem functions and services and, where applicable, cultural, spiritual, socioeconomic, and other locally relevant values (UN Convention on Biological Diversity, 2028).

[9]GEMI utilized the technological expertise of The Ocean Cleanup (www.theoceancleanup.com), an organization dedicated to removing plastics from the ocean, and "intercepting" plastics from the roughly 1,000 rivers worldwide responsible for 80% of the plastic dumped into the ocean.

[10]Most plastics in the ocean break up into very small particles of less than 0.5 mm (0.2 in) in diameter. There are two types: primary, which are manufactured microbeads, and secondary, which are degraded larger pieces of plastic (NOAA Ocean Exploration, 2040).

[11]Of special note: Kiribati financed most of the floating city projects with revenue generated by the leasing of the Enderbury Atoll to GEMI for the Earth-bound space elevator base in the late 2020s.

[12]The breeding, rearing, and harvesting of fish, shellfish, algae, and other organisms in all types of water environments. As the demand for seafood has increased, technology has made it possible to grow food in coastal marine waters and the open ocean. Aquaculture is a method used to produce food and other commercial products, restore habitat, replenish wild stocks, and rebuild populations of threatened

and endangered species (National Ocean Service, https://oceanservice.noaa.gov/facts/aquaculture.html, 2027).

[13]Large solar arrays in LEO and geosynchronous orbit collect the sun's energy and deliver it back to Earth via laser and microwave to mostly land-locked locations around the world (International Energy Agency, 2051).

GENERAL HISTORY

A few requisite chapters on our general global history illustrate significant global paradigm shifts that occurred during 2025-2055. Most notable are the pandemic of 2029-2032; terrorist attacks on the world's financial and global communications systems; and the massive investment shifts that first fueled our battle against global warming and later funded the fledgling space ecosystem.

G20 Donates Future GEMI Royalties

2027

The G20 leadership understood, as relatively wealthy countries, they would most likely never receive significant dividend returns from their GEMI stock ownership. In an uncharacteristic show of largesse, during the 2027 G20 Summit held in Quebec, Canada, then G20 President Justin Trudeau announced all G20 members had agreed to forgo any future dividends realized from the development or sale of GEMI-based technologies. Further, in a prepared statement, the G20 leadership challenged the next tier of developing nations to do the same:

"The G20 represents two-thirds of our world population and 75% of the world's trade, and we generate 85% of the world's revenue. Our focus has always been on financial growth and stability for the entire world. Towards that end, even though G20 member countries have contributed almost $800 billion to GEMI, we will still forgo our share of the potential dividend-based revenue stream from GEMI. We challenge the next economic tier of countries to do the same.

"No one can accurately predict to what extent GEMI will successfully execute its mission. However, we believe GEMI has an ambitious, idealistic set of goals, substantial financial backing, and the leadership necessary to succeed. We accept the model Mr. Fisher proposed at the 2025 Davos Summit. We want to give those countries at the bottom economic tiers every opportunity to prosper independently. We believe it is worth the gamble."

Within months of this challenge, fifty-three additional countries signed over their rights to future dividends. However, this generosity was short-lived. While GEMI began distributing dividends to member nations in 2031, each year since then, at least one country has requested that its dividends be reinstated. These requests were denied in the first few years; however, in 2034, Duarte asked the countries receiving dividends to vote on each subsequent request. To the credit of the countries already receiving dividends — despite the fact that each additional country added to the dividend pool reduced their payouts — all requests have been accepted.

Solomon Haile, President of Eritrea, explained why his country consistently voted to allow additional countries to receive dividends. "This recurring income has truly been a boon for my country. We still struggle, but our yearly income from the GEMI dividends has nearly tripled our GDP — and it grows each year," he said. "We no longer must depend on the charity of other countries, nor are we forced into one-sided partnerships with companies coveting our meager natural resources. In the spirit of the original GEMI goal to redistribute wealth, it is only right to give this opportunity to other countries."

Author's note: *A* Wall Street Journal *investigative article published in February 2029 revealed that Edward Fisher had quietly met with several of the G20 leaders before their 2027 summit in an effort to convince them to forgo future GEMI dividends. Once the G20 leadership made their announcement, Fisher methodically made the same request of at least sixty more countries, obtaining agreements from fifty-three of them to donate future dividends to the poorest countries in the world.*

The Five Days the World Was Disconnected

2029

For nearly five days in 2029, from April 5-9, more than 60% of the world was without internet service[1]. The Hack for Freedom (HFF) terrorist group claimed responsibility, and eventually, 137 of the group's members were apprehended. The International Criminal Court (ICC) found 133 members guilty of a range of charges, some as serious as first-degree murder. HFF leader Priscilla LaCombe was sentenced to life in prison without parole.

While the damage worldwide during this outage was never accurately assessed, estimates ranged from hundreds of billions of dollars to $2 trillion. And, while the number of lives lost would also never be fully quantified, direct links were established between the outage and the deaths of 1,221 people worldwide. Most of these cases were traced to internet-dependent hospitals and ambulance services, although two plane crashes, resulting in thirty-seven deaths, were also attributed to the outage.

A *New York Times* article published days after the attacks reported, "Critical business operations began to shut down within minutes of the start of the attacks, dramatically highlighting the world's dependency on internet-based data and communications. Patients within healthcare facilities and transports were hit the hardest. For nearly a week, air traffic was grounded as a result of failures in critical systems. Massive cargo ships were set adrift, having lost their ability to navigate the open seas, their crews resorting to manually steering into the closest safe harbors. Millions of mass transit and personal vehicles were rendered inoperative, cruelly exposing the vulnerabilities in the world's heavy dependence on the internet."

Six months after the attack, the Internet Corporation for Assigned Names and Numbers (ICANN) released a cyber forensics report detailing the attack methodologies used by the terrorists. The report showed more than 200 strategic physical attacks aimed to cripple the functional integrity of the global internet. On each of seven continents, major electrical grids were selectively bombed, shutting down approximately 4% of the world's electricity, all within regions where core root domain network system (DNS) servers were located. While emergency power kept these critical servers operational, they were still essentially offline because the interconnecting switches and routers in the regions were without power.

Within hours of the grid bombings, sixty-one critical submarine data cable segments in the northern Atlantic and northern Pacific oceans were bombed using explosive-laden drone submarines. Of those, fifty-three segments were entirely severed. In addition, seventeen shorter segments linking various Asian, African, and Australian regions were also attacked, with sixteen of these severed. In total, 37% of submarine data cable capacity worldwide was lost.

In addition to physically isolating or destroying many critical components of the internet, the terrorists further stressed the already compromised and diminished infrastructure with massive digital attacks. They orchestrated multiple waves of hundreds of thousands of artificial intelligence (AI) aided distributed denial-of-service (DDoS) and Border Gateway Protocol (BGP) hijacking attacks, overwhelming what was left of the routes available through the internet.

The estimated cost of the entire attack operation was in the range of $2.5 billion to $3 billion — far more than the HFF had available itself. While the HFF took credit for the attacks, it was suspected they were recruited by one or more state-funded organizations. Evidence during the ensuing trials suggested the possibility of both Saudi Arabian and Chinese involvement, although these ties were unproven.

Forbes magazine interviewed Dr. Sidney O'Hare, General Manager of IBM Security and one of the preeminent cyber security experts at the time. Referring to the efficacy of the HFF attack, O'Hare stated, "If I were asked to design a way to cripple the Internet — and I had unlimited funds — I would have used a similar methodology. They knew enough about the underlying global data infrastructure to target the destruction of specific high-density hub regions and submarine cabling systems. They then quickly and aggressively went after thwarting the inherent self-healing mechanisms that make the internet work so well. They executed what were probably millions of DDoS and BGP hijacking attacks, stopping nearly all traffic. I mean, they were good. Thankfully, they couldn't sustain that volume, and we were finally able to stop them and start the rebuild process."

It took weeks to reroute internet traffic for emergency communications and data flow. The thousands of miles of severed high-speed submarine cabling took nearly two years to repair, finally achieving average internet packet transmission speeds that approached those before the attacks.

Existing satellite-based internet services providers fared the best during the 2029 cyber terrorist attack, essentially acting as a litmus test (albeit a tragic one) for the feasibility of the space-based digital cloud we use today in the 2050s. The accelerated effort to replace Earth-bound systems with space-based satellites started soon after the attacks, and within a decade, most of the infrastructure had been shifted to more secure space systems.

Author's note: *As of 2055, the now 57-year-old LaCombe is still incarcerated in La Santé prison, Paris, France.*

---

[1]In the late 2050s, the flow of data in our world is ubiquitous. Most of us do not understand (nor do we care) how everything is connected — it just is. This "always-on" resource is realized utilizing a

heavily meshed and redundant space-based satellite hive that blankets the Earth and bi-directionally beams fast data packets directly to the trillions of devices that make up our digital world. However, through the early 2030s, critical components of the data network infrastructure called the "internet" mainly were Earth-bound, thus vulnerable to natural disasters and terrorist attacks. Physically, hundreds of thousands of networks worldwide were connected through myriad physical servers, routers, and switches. These networks were joined primarily through high-speed cabling — much of it submarine — physically connecting the continents through thousands of high-speed cabling bundles pulled along the ocean floors.

Cyberattack Breaches World Financial Systems

2030

Since the turn of the century, cyberterrorism has been a growing issue worldwide, rapidly accelerating since the early 2020s. Individuals, communities, companies, and even entire countries experienced devastating attacks. As early as 2021, United States government officials acknowledged the seriousness of cyberattacks. Jerome Powell, the Federal Reserve Chair at the time, said during a *60 Minutes* interview in April 2021, "We spend so much time and energy and money guarding against these things. There are cyberattacks every day on all major institutions now. That's a big part of the threat picture in today's world."

Through the 2020s, those behind cyberattacks became more sophisticated and, with each successful hack or ransomware payment received, more emboldened. This all came to a climax on May 7, 2030, at 12:17 am EST, when a massive, orchestrated cyberattack was launched across the global financial industry. Targeting the underlying mechanisms moving capital through local, national, and international financial institutions, tens of thousands of automated and manually coordinated cyberattacks and hacks were executed over approximately twenty-one hours. An estimated \$28 trillion was displaced across the world's financial systems during the attack. While most of this wealth was recovered, an estimated \$70 billion was never found. It took over two years to restore stability to the system.

In 2034, after several years of intense cyber-forensic investigations, an International Criminal Tribunal commission released a report describing a global consortium of cyber-criminal organizations responsible for the 2030 attacks. While hundreds of individuals were eventually arrested, the leaders and their funding source(s) were never identified.

The International Monetary Fund (IMF) said of the attacks: "Nearly 60% of the world's trusted and critical financial hubs were compromised in these attacks. It was devastating to the global economic systems, especially for those countries depending on international funding for sustenance. People died because of this attack. The world financial community must carefully reevaluate how we move international funds. We cannot afford to allow this to happen again."

As the industry sorted through the chaos that followed the attacks, security experts discovered that most critical financial industry air-gapped networks (computer networks physically isolated from other networks) had been systematically infiltrated since at least 2023. The hackers had implanted various time-synchronized Trojan horses into these (assumed) secure air-gapped networks, all timed to activate on May 7, 2030, at 12:17 am EST or shortly after. As the attacks were initiated, most of these networks were then integrated into the more extensive cyberattack. The lightning-fast, artificial intelligence–aided coordination of the massive attack kept the hackers ahead of the world's security experts for almost an entire day.

Intel Executive Vice President and Chief Architect Samantha Jones reflected in an analysis posted after the attack, "In retrospect, for decades, cybersecurity professionals had b een lulled into a dance with hackers. It was always a variation on the same theme: security hole identified; security patch applied to plug the hole. None of us considered the possibility of a years-long staging of a cyberattack that would culminate in the breach of major international financial networks once considered impregnable. The Trojan horses used ranged from hardware — memory modules mostly — to operating, security, management, and enterprise business application systems. How are we ever going to expunge this malware from the thousands of networks impacted?"

Never again would electronic currency flow so readily across cyber-borders. In the process of restoration, the concept of "short runs" was developed and instituted. These procedures allow for quantified and guaranteed values (currency) to "live" locally within regions, while providing the ability to "relocate" the value to another region of the world as part of a semi-manual transaction process that includes numerous human steps. The process is slower than previous systems but inherently more secure against cyber criminals because of the additional (manual) human component to all transactions. These transaction "pathways" have no fewer than six human-processed steps (three on each endpoint). As well, the identities of these individuals are kept anonymous, adding another layer of security to each transaction.

Author's note: *These changes in the world's financial systems have stood the test of time, and as of the writing of this book (2056), they are still employed and have yet to be compromised in any but minor instances.*

Regionalism Takes Hold around the World

2033

Throughout history, humans have traded for goods and services, exchanging everything from handshakes to trillions of dollars' worth of electronic transactions pulsing every day through the world's financial centers, to close the deal.

For decades leading up to the 2020s, we continued to refine these models, becoming increasingly comfortable with — and dependent on — the maturing global economic community. We began relying more on sources from around the world for large portions of our energy, food, and water (EFW) needs. Nonetheless, by the mid-2030s, strategic regional EFW zones[1], motivated by the need to ensure local EFW security for the people of the region, began to form around the world.

Most social and economic scientists agree that four events precipitated this global economic contraction and geographic isolation: two pandemics and two global terrorist attacks. These events led to the formation of thousands of small and large, essentially self-sufficient regional EFW zones, and the predominately regional approach to day-to-day life and commerce we have in the mid-2050s.

The global pandemics erupted at the beginning and the end of the 2020s. The first, lasting from 2020-2023, was caused by the coronavirus SARS-CoV-2 (COVID-19). The second, brought on by the highly contagious airborne strain of the Langya henipavirus (LayV), began early in 2029, and although the world's governments were better prepared this time around, it still lasted three years.

As this second pandemic was building momentum, on April 5, 2030, the cyber-terrorist group, Hack for Freedom, unleased an aggressive global attack on the Internet, crippling the worldwide communications system. It took five days to stop the attack and years to fully recover. A short month later, on May 7, the world's financial markets experienced an unrelated, highly coordinated cyberattack, causing temporary displacement of tens of trillions of dollars and the permanent loss of nearly $70 billion.

During each of the pandemics, countries shut down their borders to slow the virus's spread. With fewer trade routes across national and international borders, and the world's financial and communications systems in shambles, there were no viable paths to return to the pre-2029 model, further reenforcing the growing shift to regionalism.

In the wake of these devastating pandemics, an estimated 6.3 million people died (World Health Organization, 2033). In addition, the interdependent global economy was severely curtailed, reducing or eliminating entire industries and causing the loss of millions of jobs. Indeed, a 2035 International Monetary Fund (IMF) report estimated these four unrelated events together cost the global community $37 trillion. They revealed the frailties of our globally interdependent healthcare, financial, and communications systems and exposed the inadequacies of our staid solutions for living, working, and trading across international borders. Leaders around the world began to reevaluate their level of participation in the global economic community — and whether strategic regional partnerships might better ensure the security of their populations' ongoing EFW needs and make them less susceptible to periodic catastrophic global disruptions.

Indeed, the joint statement issued during the closing meeting of the November 2032 G20 Summit, held in Brasília, Brazil, addressed this regional phenomenon and presented a clear recommendation to world leaders. A segment reads: "For the next several years, our global and regional leaders need to focus more on national quality of life; energy, food, and water security; and CO_2 emission-reducing projects, and less on lofty international economic goals. We need to foster bidirectional cooperative learning and training to ensure we all can efficiently build new and relevant infrastructures and EFW best practices. In our opinion, we will only see enduring, positive results if we can rebuild our infrastructures and environments, while retraining ourselves in new practices that align with a reduced demand on our natural ecosystems."

French Prime Minister Yannick Jadot described the mood of most world leaders at the time, stating, "There were just too many catastrophic events — man-made and natural — impacting the world. Extreme weather, cyberattacks on individuals, corporations, and government systems, malicious mass-media misinformation… it was frenzied, an epidemic. We all were stepping back somewhat."

By the early 2030s, most governments were shifting their priorities to ensure the long-term local availability of renewable energy sources, clean water, adequate food supplies, and extreme-weather resistant shelters for their people. Among the resources they relied on to help with these goals was the World Biosphere Protection Treaty (WBPT), ratified in 2028. While WBPT programs were limited to the preservation of key world resources, by this time, hundreds of billions of WBPT dollars were flowing into all regions of the world, most well aligned with the EFW goals of those same regions.

Another new initiative (still extensively utilized in the 2050s) was the Regional EFW Zone System[2] (REZS), developed by GEMI. Dr. Hana Duarte explained why GEMI built this system: "By 2035, EFW regionalism had already left the station. GEMI had centers in most of these regional EFW zones, and we probably had hundreds of energy, food, water, and habitat projects already in the works. So, the decision to create this tool was easy. Get this: The idea for REZS came from a GEMI data scientist, Dr. Millie Brown, who modeled the system after a survivalist homestead computer game she played as a kid. She explained how she had to figure out how much of everything was needed to survive, and where she could get these things locally. If she did a good job, she survived. If she didn't, she had to find another source and pay whatever it took. Sound familiar?"

In fact, the next decade would witness a steady increase in the number of EFW zones worldwide. The *Wall Street Journal* stated in a 2041 market analysis, "Energy, food, water, and shelter security has always been a priority for governments of the world. However, as the regionalist movement has steadily grown, world leaders have correspondingly increased spending on the components needed to meet this shift in trade strategy. In fact, the interzone trade activity across the top hundred regional EFW zones worldwide dropped an average of 23% between 2030 and 2040, while capital spending related to enhancing each zone's food, water, and shelter security more than doubled for the same period."

The *New York Times* memorialized the 2020s in a retrospective article published in the summer of 2031, stating, "The previous decade might be best remembered as 'The Resilient 2020s.'" Certainly, recovering from two worldwide pandemics and two global terrorist attacks within a ten-year span affirms this title. While few deny the hardships the world endured during this turbulent decade in our shared history, this period also resulted in systemic changes in many of our global society's norms, some of which, twenty-five years later, are still in force. Certainly, EFW regionalism has thrived into the 2050s, demonstrating the positive benefits of this new model of living.

----

[1]Strategic Regional EFW Zones are defined as geo-political regions around the world whose member countries are dedicated to shared energy, food, and water independence within the zone. Zone partner countries share responsibility to ensure EFW security for all within the zone.

[2]The Regional EFW Zone System is an open-source computer system developed in the 2030s and maintained by GEMI. REZS assists leaders in regional EFW zones in the development of clear, strategic, and actionable, plans to realize EFW independence within their zones.

REZS is used in hundreds of regional zones around the world in the mid-2050s.

Artificial Intelligence

2035

At New York-Presbyterian Hospital on August 7, 2035, one of the last psychological barriers to using artificial intelligence (AI) was shattered with the first successful surgeon-free, AI-driven robotic surgery to replace a biological human heart with a mechanical heart. While surgeons were in attendance, three synchronized surgical robots guided by an AI cardiac surgery performance system performed the entire surgical procedure. Developed with knowledge collected from thousands of cardiac surgeons, nurses, and anesthesiologists over ten years, the system worked flawlessly, completing the surgery in two hours and forty-seven minutes.

Dr. H Jiang, MD, PhD, an internationally known cardiac surgeon and the Surgical Director of Heart Failure, Heart Transplantation, and Mechanical Circulatory Support programs at New York-Presbyterian Hospital, led the team. He said, "This is such an important milestone in the evolution of AI and robotics in critical healthcare. We have successfully demonstrated the power of these tools in performing one of the most complex of operations. There's still much work to do, but this model will eventually allow us to care for many more people in need, regardless of where they live or the availability of specially trained healthcare professionals."

The ubiquitous use of AI has been a holy grail since the early 1950s and the advent of the first computer programming language. However, it was not until the mid-2030s that the world began to embrace AI fully in our business, healthcare, community, and personal lives. By this time, decades of continual AI programming refinements, increases in supercomputing processing speeds, and near-infinite universal bandwidth finally began to unleash the long-promised capabilities of AI. The short-lived generative artificial intelligence (GAI)[1] boom of the 2020s spurred the development of stringent global policies developed to guide the responsible use of AI. This gave people both the framework and the comfort level needed to trust and enlist AI systems in more fundamental, historically human-only tasks.

Virtually no industries were untouched by AI. While artificial general intelligence (AGI)[2] remained elusive until the McCracken dense biological array[3] stunned the world in 2038, millions of AI applications were developed throughout the 2030s and 2040s, allowing for more complex uses of AI.

Deep space colonization has been especially receptive to AI. Certainly, AI has been necessary for maintaining safe and acceptable living and work conditions within space colonies for nearly two decades. Motivated both by the complexity of the operations that need to be performed in space and by the chronic shortage of skilled people, the aggressive development of AI systems has continued, helping to ensure colonists and workers can safely thrive in space environments devoid of human-based advanced support. A 2038 excerpt from an AI industry analysis in *Space Investments*, affirming the vast commercial potential of one specific type of AI in space, states, "Our money is on Artificial Narrow Intelligence (ANI)[4] for at least the next decade. For ANI systems in space, we estimate a revenue stream of $7 trillion by 2040, rivaling the perennial red-hot materials, propulsion, and food markets. Why? Because ANI systems are essential for space colonies and corporations to function, and for their colonists and workers to survive. The air these people breathe, the nutrients they consume, their healthcare, the monolithic systems that orchestrate the daily functioning and communications within each space colony — almost everything depends on AI systems and their eclectic army of robotic helpers."

Indeed, AI systems are as expensive as they are necessary. For many of these systems, gathering the required knowledge and decision-making logic, and developing the actual AI systems themselves, can involve thousands of subject matter experts and dozens of companies, costing billions of dollars and taking years to complete. Add robotics equipment to this, and the cost can skyrocket into the tens of billions. Still, since the mid-2040s, we can, with a reasonable level of confidence, use AI systems to live and work in space without depending on humans with specialized skills to be nearby.

Author's note: Throughout the 2040s, the development of AI and robotics systems has seen a systemic shift from Earth-based to space enterprises. This trend has tracked closely with the migration of skilled developers to space colonies. As of 2055, nearly 85% of AI and robotics systems purchased or leased for use in space were developed in space.

---

[1] GAI is capable of generating text, images, or other media, using generative models. Generative AI models learn the patterns and structure of their input training data and then generate new data that has similar characteristics (Wikipedia, 2023).

[2] AGI involves the ability of an AI agent to learn, perceive, understand, and function entirely like a human being ("Seven Types of Artificial Intelligence," *Forbes* magazine, 2045).

[3] A cutting-edge, biology-based AGI model developed collaboratively by the Massachusetts Institute of Technology in the United States and Tsinghua University in China that was famously unveiled on February 13, 2038, at the International Artificial Intelligence Summit in Paris. However, within months of the event, the system was shut down because of detected unauthorized specialized cell development and propagation (memory and storage). The "machine" seemingly took the initiative to improve its internal processing and storage capabilities. While other biology-based AI systems have been developed, the McCracken array is still contained and studied within an air-gapped environment (*ANI/Robotics Journal*, 2039).

[4]ANI systems can only perform a specific task autonomously using human-like capabilities ("Seven Types of Artificial Intelligence," *Forbes* magazine, 2045).

A New Capitalism Takes Hold

2036

By the mid-2030s, a new capitalism model had taken root in most regions of the world. This model extended the traditional corporate goals — maximizing profits and satisfying shareholders — to stewardship of other stakeholders, including employees, communities, and the environment. While brought on by a decades-long confluence of events, both GEMI and IMPF were significant drivers of this movement. By 2035, the two organizations together controlled approximately $38 trillion. Collectively, they had thousands of offices and research facilities and millions of employees and interns from almost every country in the world. Although their missions were different, they worked alongside government and business leaders worldwide to pursue common goals.

Both GEMI and IMPF, from their inceptions, committed material, time, and capital to their stakeholders in a way that would become the gold standard for corporate responsibility and a model for what was then called a "new capitalism." Edward Fisher and Dr. Hana Duarte, recognizing the need for a new organizational model, understood the opportunity and their responsibilities to instill it into their respective organizations and to foster this corporate model and culture worldwide.

While Fisher and Dr. Duarte worked together on the model, most historians credit Dr. Duarte and her expertise in cultural anthropology for the cultural framework eventually routinized within GEMI and IMPF. She orchestrated and nurtured the development of the overarching GEMI culture and policies. She systematically encouraged similar corporate behavior in the thousands of predominately local businesses with which GEMI interacted within its hundred-plus centers and thousands of satellite offices worldwide.

In her keynote speech at the World Trade Organization's Annual Summit in 2036, Dr. Duarte explained the GEMI community approach. "We feel strongly the need to participate in the communities we're a part of. For GEMI, this means embracing hundreds of subcultures worldwide. Our GEMI culture, I believe, has distilled the best of this spectrum of cultural attributes, and we've made these our own," she said. "We've learned the importance of looking out for each other, our local community, and the environment — and we expect the same sensitivity from our many business partners. Care for your employees and show them respect, contribute time and capital to your communities, use local labor, buy local material, help in times of crisis. These tenets are so basic, so right. Of course, we're going to encourage these practices."

Fisher underscored Dr. Duarte's sentiment, noting the similarities of the IMPF philosophy. "This expanded inclusiveness has to be woven into the fabric of our corporate identity and culture — not an add-on after all of the shareholders have eaten their fill. From day one, IMPF becomes a responsible corporate citizen of each city we do a project with," he said. "Look at our historical record on this. We never walk away from a city. Once we have engaged, and to the extent we're allowed and able, we commit to stewardship of the city and its citizens. Likewise, we truly consider our employees to be family — a huge family. We take care of each other. It's the right way to do things."

At the annual 2037 GEMI Summit, keynote guest speaker Fabiola Gulotta, CEO of EpochSpace, the first space media company not owned by an Earth-bound media company, recognized Fisher and Dr. Duarte for their contributions to the evolution of capitalism: "GEMI and IMPF leadership have played active roles in crafting a new model for how a corporation should develop and maintain its relationship with shareholders and stakeholders alike. The world is a better place because of their unwavering focus on fairness for all shareholders, employees, and local communities."

Where the Money Came From: Investment Shifts through the Years

2025 – 2055

Through the three decades leading up to the 2050s, vast amounts of investment capital were funneled first into developing alternative energy sources and CO_2 emission-reducing infrastructure projects and then, more recently, into space colonization and exploration. The United Nations Conference on Trade and Development (UNCTAD) 2045 *World Investment Report* estimated that as of 2045, more than $63 trillion had been spent on these energy, urban infrastructure, and space projects during this period. This unprecedented funding enabled profound, systemic changes both here on Earth and in space, blunting the more severe effects of global warming and fueling the early space ecosystem development we are still witnessing in the late 2050s.

What pool of investors was responsible for this focused, aggressive capital infusion? Economists point to the then-emerging younger generations of individual and institutional investors, traders, bankers, and money managers. This group grew up with the specter of irreversible catastrophic environmental changes wrought by their elders. They were understandably more receptive to socially responsible investing (SRI) in companies adhering to environmental, social, and governance (ESG) frameworks. They demonstrated a preference to invest in companies such as IMPF, with its unprecedented funding to remediate urban infrastructures; BlackRock, with its expansive ESG fund portfolio; and other socially responsible organizations.

Forbes magazine, in a 2019 article titled "Generational Wealth in America," described how "…[American] Baby Boomers, the generation of people born between 1944 and 1964, are expected to transfer $30 trillion in wealth to younger generations over the next many years. This jaw-dropping amount has led many journalists and financial experts to refer to the gradual event as the 'great wealth transfer.'" With the rest of the world factored in, this number balloons to an estimated $70 trillion.

Linda Williams, an analyst for *The Economist*, described the importance of this shift in a February 2043 article, "Cyclic Generational Wealth." Williams wrote, "The late '20s through the '30s brought an alignment of opportunity with need. Tens of trillions of dollars in generational wealth shifted from baby boomers to millennials at a critical time when worldwide global warming remediations needed to begin in earnest. At the risk of sounding hyperbolic, this unprecedented wealth transfer to younger, more socially responsible investors worldwide likely saved humanity."

By the late 2030s, the Global Environmental Monitoring System (GEMS)reported that roughly 65% of large urban infrastructure projects were within acceptable CO_2 standards, and, as such, were considered completed. As the number of these mega-projects declined, investment capital began to shift to emerging opportunities in space[1]. Space colonization and exploration, as the *Wall Street Journal* described in a 2039 investment analysis, is the "last grand frontier — one with no discernible limits." The *WSJ* continued, "The world is fascinated with everything space. The second space elevator was completed in eastern Africa last year, and a South American elevator is scheduled to go live before the end of 2041, ensuring the necessary materials and consumables will flow more quickly to space colonies. These conduits, coupled with dozens of daily commercial spaceplane flights, are making it easy to get people and materials to space. It's like something out of a science-fiction themed Wild West."

Deep space exploration and colonization, together with a cleaner, more balanced existence here on Earth, gave people (including investors) hope and confidence in a brighter future. As the space ecosystem evolves into the late-2050s, opportunities will continue to entice large amounts of capital from Earth-based investors into those corporations shooting for the stars.

---

[1]The staged dissolution of IMPF between 2047 and 2052 added an estimated \$35 trillion to this immense investment shift from Earth-based CO_2 remediation to space ecosystem development.

SPACE EXPLORATION AND COLONIZATION

Dr. Jacob Baptista had a clear, practical vision and roadmap for the future of space exploration and colonization. This, coupled with GEMI's broad scientific expertise and hundreds of billions of dollars in targeted funding, were major contributors to building a viable foundation for the space ecosystem in place today. GEMI continues to work alongside thousands of innovative companies contributing to the ongoing evolution of humans in space.

Baptista on the Importance of Space Exploration and Colonization

2049

Shortly before Dr. Jacob Baptista's retirement in 2050, the 2049 United Nations Space Consortium Conference (UN-SCC) committee invited him to set the tone of their annual conference by writing a short essay on the importance of space exploration and colonization. Below is the conference introduction of Dr. Baptista, followed by his essay.

With two Nobel Prizes to his credit and nearly three decades as Chief Science Officer for GEMI, Dr. Jacob Baptista is arguably one of the most influential thinkers of the twenty-first century. During his twenty-six-year tenure, Dr. Baptista and an army of GEMI scientists, engineers, and interns left their mark on Earth and in space. However, it is Dr. Baptista's vision of our future in space, realized by GEMI space-based science and funding, that has become synonymous with space exploration and colonization.

Under Dr. Baptista's leadership, GEMI spent $250 billion (in 2030 dollars) to build the world's first space elevator, creating a new world wonder and a reliable conduit to transport supplies from Earth to space quickly and economically. In the process, GEMI developed methodologies to mass manufacture the incredibly strong, lightweight, graphene sheathing in space, a key component in constructing safer space transport vehicles and colonies.

In addition, GEMI invested hundreds of billions of dollars in R&D for their center-based space technologies and for specific, strategically aligned space technology companies. Together, they developed next-generation spaceplanes, components of space colonies, resource-rich asteroid mining capabilities, and best practices in space construction techniques, ensuring the foundations of our fledgling space ecosystem were in place.

Dr. Baptista, GEMI, and other pioneering space companies paved the way for the robust space ecosystem now in place. They laid the foundation vital to our continued space colonization and exploration. For that, we will be forever grateful.

Why Space?

— Dr. Jacob Baptista

We have learned and accomplished so much during these last few decades here on Mother Earth. We are no longer dependent on fossil fuels. We are more frugal and thoughtful with the resources we continue to consume. Our forests are more abundant and our oceans cleaner. Within a few years, we will most likely attain our net-zero CO_2 emissions goal. Truly, on many fronts, Earth's biosphere is healing.

We are finding new ways to house and feed ourselves. We have made huge headways with ocean habitats and food farms. Take projects like Bangladesh's vast semi-submerged water habitat clusters[1] along the coast of Chittagong, already with over one million inhabitants. Or regenerative ocean farming (ROF), now the leading global source of shellfish and nutrient-rich plant-based consumables. Looking forward, we have justifiable hope for a healthy future.

So, why not just continue along our hard-earned and sustainable path here on Earth? Why space?

Because, viscerally, humans need to reach for the stars. We have an innate curiosity that has always compelled us to explore the unknown, collect more knowledge, seek new challenges. These human qualities are baked into the genes of the nine billion souls now crowding our small planet. Add to this the practical need for an escape route, of sorts, if a catastrophic event on Earth rendered it no longer suitable for human life. It's abundantly clear: Space is the answer.

I am often asked how the next few decades of space exploration and colonization will play out. I used to suggest we look to science fiction for a peek into what directions space colonization and societies will take (so many of our technological advances begin as sci-fi). But now I suggest we read today's space-based business, research, and cultural news articles for insights. The enormous potential impacts of the space ecosystem on business, science, and society defy the imagination. Millions of people and hundreds of trillions of dollars will flow into our still-emerging space ecosystem within the next decade alone. Like the Industrial Revolution that began nearly 300 years ago, our exodus to space will likewise change and expand our world, bringing opportunities — and perils — we cannot fathom in the present.

This slow migration to space to live, work, and explore will continue unabated for decades. We will build colonies on other celestial bodies, but most will be space-anchored[2] in low- and middle-Earth orbits (LEO and MEO) — at least as long as Earth is the primary source of life-sustaining supplies and support. However, once Spacers[3] become self-sufficient, capable of gathering all the resources necessary to sustain life from asteroids and other space sources, the game will change. Earth's umbilical cord will be cut, and we will accelerate our explorations deeper into space. I suspect we are only looking at another twenty years before this happens. Indeed, many countries and corporations are already planning and developing policies and technologies in anticipation of this next chapter in space exploration.

Deeper into space. For some of us, this is a thrilling prospect. Most, however, will elect to stay on Earth or close enough to travel to and from space efficiently and quickly. Still, once we have the freedom and the means to move further from Mother Earth, many of us will jump at the opportunity. Our curiosity will continue to drive us, now profoundly untethered from Earth, to travel further into the unknown, collecting yet more knowledge and chasing more new challenges. For now, though, we still have plenty of work ahead of us to ensure stable and confident steps in our grand space evolution.

---

[1]Models of community living and working in habitats anchored off coastal freshwater and ocean settings. Developed by GEMI and other companies, by 2055, approximately 160 million people were living in these communities worldwide.

[2]This condition occurs when an artificial satellite/colony/spaceship is locked (anchored) into a specific orbit.

[3]Individuals and families living or working in space colonies for open-ended, extended periods.

GEMI Announces Space Elevator Project

2026

In the spring of 2026, GEMI held a press conference announcing their plans to build a space elevator on the Enderbury Atoll, within the island nation of Kiribati, by 2036 at an estimated cost of $210 billion. During the announcement, lead scientist Dr. Jacob Baptista explained, "We need a safe, reliable, clean, and inexpensive way to transport massive amounts of material from Earth to space — and not just for GEMI projects. The space elevator is a key component to meeting our short-term goals of building the Earth-to-outer-space infrastructure and the ecosystem needed to further humanity's drive to explore space. We will partner with academic and commercial research and development labs worldwide to ensure we employ the best minds and technologies for the project. We will also utilize the International Space Station and have already committed to a long-term lease agreement to use a portion of the ISS to house our early space-based elevator operations."

The concept of a space elevator that extends 22,000 miles up from Earth's surface to an endpoint in geosynchronous orbit[1] has been around since at least 1895, when Russian scientist Konstantin Tsiolkovsky created a model describing how such a machine might work. Since then, the model, mathematics, and technologies involved in building a space elevator have received periodic updates from numerous scientists, corporations, and government agencies. Still, it was not until Dr. Baptista decided the space elevator was a crucial component to meeting the space and Mars-related goals of GEMI that the necessary capital and expertise were committed to making the space elevator a reality.

Many leaders in government and business considered a space elevator the best hope for wholesale entrance into space. In fact, until the mid-2020s, numerous government agencies and corporations worldwide were still seriously researching the feasibility of constructing one themselves. However, by 2027, Dr. Baptista's team of engineers and scientists on the project was growing, enticed from many would-be competitors to join the GEMI effort because of the unprecedented resources GEMI and Dr. Baptista had committed to building an elevator. While officially protesting these personnel defects to GEMI, most governments and corporations with these aspirations were happy to step aside and allow GEMI to build (and pay for) the first-generation space elevator. They rightly assumed subsequent elevators would be less costly, building on lessons learned and technologies developed within the GEMI project.

While most of the technologies needed to construct a space elevator existed at the time of Dr. Baptista's announcement, there were no solutions for mass-producing the reinforced graphene cabling needed for the elevator tether system. However, by 2030, GEMI researchers had succeeded in manufacturing graphene in large enough quantities in a specially constructed pressurized module added to the ISS. In addition to this breakthrough, the GEMI/ISS-based graphene cabling operation was the first large-scale manufacturing facility in space. With the graphene cabling milestone met, Dr. Baptista's team worked through the project's remaining components, and the historic GEMI space elevator became operational in 2035.

Two additional space elevators were constructed by 2041. The first of these was a collaborative project between GEMI and fifty-one African countries at a price tag of $43 billion. The anchor for this elevator was constructed 189 miles off the coast of Kenya. The second elevator was a collaboration among thirteen South American nations. The South American space elevator anchor was constructed 152 miles off the coast of Ecuador. At the cost of $71 billion, this elevator was nearly twice as fast and had a 40% larger cargo capacity than the two earlier systems. Both collaboratives involved trade agreements among the member nations sharing the elevator and the revenue it generated.

Author's note: GEMI would eventually spend $252 billion to build the first space elevator — more than twice the cost of the next two elevators constructed. While there have been several more extensive projects in the last two decades, the price tag for the GEMI elevator was unprecedented at the time, exceeding the $150 billion cost to build the International Space Station (ISS), another ambitious space project of the early 2000s. As well, the total cost of the space elevator was covered by GEMI as a single private corporation, not a consortium of nations as was the case with the ISS.

[1]A geosynchronous orbit (GEO) is a prograde, low inclination orbit about Earth having a period of 23 hours 56 minutes 4 seconds. A spacecraft in geosynchronous orbit appears to remain above Earth at a constant longitude, although it may seem to wander north and south. The spacecraft returns to the same point in the sky at the same time each day. (NASA, 2055)

Individual Space Habitats (ISH) Introduced

Up through the late 2020s, the goal of prolonged (i.e., more than one year) routine living and working in space had been prohibitive due to numerous and significant system challenges. Such challenges included radiation exposure, the need for a sustainable food supply, the lack of an efficient and inexpensive method for transporting supplies and people to/from space, and the imperative to create an enclosed human environment conducive to long-term "casual" living and working. However, the confluence of scientific breakthroughs and new technologies in the decade leading up to the 2030s eventually made this goal a reality.

GEMI, along with numerous business partners, introduced its first attempt at building acceptable living quarters for space in 2028. The GEMI vessel was a prolate spheroid, much like an American football. Dubbed a "pod" by the GEMI research team who designed it, this individual space habitat (ISH) contained approximately 9,000 square feet of livable space. Approximately 6,000 square feet were designed and reserved for residential living and work. The remaining 3,000 square feet housed systems that were needed to maintain the ISH and life support for its inhabitants. The ISH was designed for mass production entirely in space.

Unlike the elaborate ISH-like space residences and communities of the 2050s, the early ISH models had only basic functionality and limited long-term life support systems. The hydroponics system integrated well with unit air and sewage systems, creating an adequate closed ecosystem. However, unlike the robust, fully automated systems to come, the core hydroponics system required daily manual maintenance and needed to be infused with new nutrient bundles twice yearly to maintain optimal nutrient output for the inhabitants.

Quality oxygen production/circulation systems were also a challenge not fully resolved until later models. Early inhabitants (mostly scientists and interns) often complained of the strong, musty smell in the air. As well, early models were not built to protect against certain types of deep space radiation, such as galactic cosmic rays. As a result, these models were limited to deployment in near-Earth orbits only. They also still utilized combustion-based propulsion. Hydrogen-powered systems were not incorporated in ISH designs until 2041. Also, the early models had no "direct-connect" capability for joining a hub (a community cluster), thus limiting their ability to join other communities dynamically. Until the mid-2030s, joining an ISH to a hub required a prolonged spacewalk by at least three workers to manually connect the two vessels.

The parts for the first deployed GEMI ISH were sent up to the International Space Station (ISS) via conventional rocket and assembled from the ISS. This first ISH was extended from the ISS on a tether in June 2028. After extensive testing, six additional ISHs were deployed from the ISS later that same year. This maiden artificial gravity "colony" was connected to the first operational hub, Taurus. It was then untethered, officially becoming the first independent, space-based GEMI Center (christened The Pleiades) in January 2029. Even with its limitations, the first ISH was considered a technological marvel at the time.

First GEMI-led Moon Landing and Colony

2029

On December 21, 2029, a broad collaboration of countries, companies, and investors, led by Dr. Baptista and partially funded by GEMI, launched an ambitious mission to establish a small permanent human colony on the Moon. A total of six crew members — Mission Commander Dr. Jillian Badala; Pilot Dr. Makena Achebe, Mission Specialists Dr. Albert McVie, Dr. Bethany Noll, and Jim Bower; and Landing Specialist Dr. Sophia Perez — successfully entered the Moon's orbit on December 24. On Christmas Day, all six crew members went down to the Moon's surface in the lunar ship, the Raven, while the command module remained in orbit for the duration of the mission.

For 127 days, the crew lived and worked on the lunar surface, first building the temporary colony habitat, and then assembling the infrastructure needed to sustain the colony as it grew in subsequent missions. To protect against the dangerous levels of radiation on the surface due to the Moon's thin atmosphere, permanent colony structures were built at least five meters below the lunar surface. Using a lightweight backhoe delivered in one of three earlier supply shipments, they dug a twenty-meter deep, elongated trench. They then moved three satellite containers (previously used to land supplies for the mission) into the trench and connected them. The two means of egress from the underground units to the lunar surface were through large diameter angled conduits, complete with molded steps. Once all systems were tested and verified active, they covered the habitats, leaving only the conduits exposed.

After completing the living quarters, thirty-seven days after landing, four crew members moved to the underground colony, while two remained in the temp hab. They spent their remaining time on the Moon performing hundreds of tests and assembling the infrastructure-related components necessary for long-term colonization.

This successful manned Moon mission came on the heels of the US NASA Artemis program's delayed human-crewed landing on the Moon in the fall of 2029. But not all in the industry reacted positively to the GEMI-led mission. NASA Systems Administrator William McKinney called it "reckless and irresponsibly premature." In response, the director of the Brazilian space program Agência Espacial Brasileira (AEB), Dr. Hector Souza, explained, "Our [the collaborative's] lunar program was an international team effort and was not in competition with any national or commercial space programs. Our agenda, goals, and timelines were clearly stated, and safety for all involved was always our top priority. While we appreciate NASA's decades-long contributions to space exploration, we will build on this collaboration and continue to contribute to space colonization, both on the Moon and elsewhere. I have no doubt we will continue to succeed."

Dr. Baptista, in a CNN interview shortly after the crew landed back on Earth, exclaimed, "I must say, I so enjoyed working on this project for the past three years. We freely used expertise and technologies from seventeen countries and dozens of companies. Funding poured in from individuals and organizations. We [GEMI] had guaranteed the funding, but, surprisingly, the mission only cost us about $11 billion. I mean, for most of the companies involved in the project, this amounted to a validation of their technologies. Not a lot of money exchanged hands for this one."

Later in the interview, Dr. Baptista was asked about the NASA Artemis program's ultimate goal of landing and establishing a small colony of humans on Mars and how this might conflict with similar GEMI goals. He answered, "This was an international, cooperative effort for us. At best, GEMI is a catalyst for getting humanity fired up about getting our butts to Mars — and beyond. We're just going to keep moving along our timeline, with the help of our partners. Establishing a Moon-based colony is an important first step, but we're not quite there yet. We will monitor the radiation levels and life support systems in the colony habitats for a few months, and if safe, we have another launch scheduled for mid- next year to shuttle another six people to the Moon colony to live and work for a few months. Still, our mission and focus are more on Mars and open space colonization. As exciting as establishing a Moon-based human colony was, let's all look to Mars and to getting a human colony established there now. As you know, we already have a manned mission to Mars scheduled for December of 2031 only two years from now!"

The Space Colony Hub

2030

Safety has always been the top priority for humans living and working in space. Hubs, from the beginning, were designed to supply artificial gravity, redundant systems, and emergency life support to their attached ISHs. Hubs rotate along their axes, creating centrifugal forces simulating gravity within the ISHs that range from near zero-gravity to forces exceeding Earth's natural gravitational load. Hubs are also spacecraft, and along with their connected ISHs, most hub systems can leave Earth's orbit, accelerate, and travel, albeit slowly, in open space. Also, in the case of an abort-level emergency, while ISHs do not have the requisite shielding for re-entry to Earth, hubs do. After moving all ISH inhabitants into a hub, the hub can then disconnect the attached ISHs, descend through the Earth's atmosphere, and land in a body of water.

ISH/hub connectors are standardized, allowing ISHs to move from one hub colony to another. Most ISHs have enough propulsion and navigational capabilities to perform these basic maneuvers. While ISHs are physically connected to just one hub, a hub can stand alone or bond with one or more other hubs to create larger colonies. Bonded hubs communicate through encrypted radio signals uniquely identifying each hub, its purpose, and the larger colony community to which they are bound. Colony sizes range from one hub with one attached ISH to hundreds of hubs with thousands of ISHs, creating large living and work communities with populations in the tens of thousands.

Far from the diverse ecosystems that make up the myriad space colonies in the 2050s, the first few colonies comprised single hubs with no more than eight attached ISHs. One of the first operational hubs, Taurus, was a 200-meter-long, relatively flat, oblate spheroid ship. It had seven attached ISHs and was limited to near-Earth orbits only. Its maximum rotation rate could not generate a gravitational force of more than 50% of Earth's gravity. In comparison, a typical, present-day (2055) hub system can exceed 2,000 meters in length, with up to five ISH-filled rings along its axis, each rotating at a different rate based on functional gravitational need.

These early primitive colonies bore little resemblance to the colony monoliths of the 2050s. However, with the opening of the second and third space elevators in 2039 and 2041, materials and technologies could more readily be transported to space. The space colony ecosystem evolved quickly in the next several years as hundreds of companies scrambled to meet the demands for personal, communal, and commercial colony systems. This massive push into space also accelerated the migration of people to space to live and work. A 2055 space census estimated that nearly three million humans now live and work in space colonies.

The number of colonies increased tenfold between 2045 and 2055 alone, now numbering approximately 2,600 colony communities. While most of these colony complexes are social and commercial hives of activity similar to thriving small towns on Earth, the 2050s have experienced a growth in mega-colonies unimagined just a decade before, with many rivaling small Earth-bound cities in size and complexity. Ranging in population from 10,000 to 50,000, most of the mega-colonies owe their existence to corporations and universities, while the largest are elaborately sponsored extensions of Earth-bound countries.

An Early Private Space Colony

2033

By the late 2030s, the space colony ecosystem had begun to expand. The inexpensive transportation of perishables, building materials, technologies, and people to space had become routinized, thanks to the advent of space elevators, commercial SSTO spaceplanes, and very fast reusable short-haul spaceships. This, coupled with space-harvested and manufactured construction material, consumables, and fuel, cut the cost of building a space colony to approximately 25% of that of just a few years prior. At that time, even a single hub with a few ISHs could exceed $80 billion (in 2030 US dollars) to build, and another $4 billion to $5 billion per year to maintain. This was more than most organizations could afford or were willing to risk for an uncertain return.

To mitigate their financial exposure, those private and government organizations seeking to establish an early presence in space formed partnerships with other like-minded entities. This standard business practice allowed them to share the construction and maintenance costs to reduce the risks of developing a colony. Specialized investment tools to finance the highly speculative cost of early space colony development and space exploration were quickly advanced by large financial institutions. Even so, the level of long-term financial commitment and the inherent risks allowed only partners with very deep and stable cash reserves to participate.

One of the first private contracted space colonies was built by Axiom Space (AS) and GEMI[1] for the SpaceEd Group, a pioneering consortium of sixteen universities seeking to establish a permanent academic presence in space. Led by Massachusetts Institute of Technology (MIT), Harvard University, California Institute of Technology (Caltech), and Stanford University, each partner had the requisite long-term stable funding. Indeed, with nearly $900 billion in combined assets (in 2030 US dollars) in their endowment funds, the founding members of the SpaceEd Group were easily able to finance entry into early space colony development.

MIT, Harvard, Caltech, and Stanford contributed $5 billion each and were each allotted an entire ISH unit (approximately 12,000 square feet of habitable quarters by that time). Each of the remaining twelve institutions contributed $2.5 billion and was assigned 50% of one of the remaining six units. The initial cash outlay for the universities was $50 billion, with a twenty-year lease commitment. The first occupants arrived in the fall of 2033, and by the new year, all sixteen universities had taken possession of their accommodations. At that time, the SpaceEd colony housed 60 university staff, professors, and students. Together with seventeen permanent colony crew members, they lived and worked in ten ISHs attached to one hub, orbiting 342 miles above the surface of Earth.

Dr. Barbara Greenwood, an astrophysicist from Caltech, describes what she saw approaching the SpaceEd colony for the first time: "Coming up on the colony, I saw the university logos prominently displayed on their ISHs — it was powerful imagery. I remember thinking we had finally committed to space, and we were even advertising there!"

In addition to GEMI's Pleiades and the SpaceEd colonies, between 2030 and 2035 (when the GEMI space elevator became operational), only six additional artificial gravity generating space colonies[2] were built. AS/GEMI owned two, which were used for space tourists and short-term business- and science-related leasing. As well, OA/GEMI developed three of the other four colonies. Two were under government contracts by NASA and the European Space Agency (ESA), and one was a speculative colony developed for a group of investors to use for early space manufacturing-related businesses. The fourth was Yuánzhùtǐ, a cylindricalcolony[3] spaceship built by China.

Author's note: Over the next twenty years, the SpaceEd Colony would flourish as a space-based academic hub, with numerous member universities expanding their space-based footprint to include outposts on the Moon, Mars, and beyond.

As a member of this group, MIT achieved a footnote in space history as the first academic space entity registered in the UN's new system created to track space-based assets of Earth-bound organizations and governments. MIT's ISH United Nations Tracked Space Assets (UNTSA) was assigned number ACA000000000001MIT.

----

[1]From its inception, GEMI partnered (usually through large equity investments and shared intellectual property (IP)) with other companies to further its mission on Earth and in space. Its long partnership with Axiom Space (AS) centered around the research, development, and construction of hub and spoke space colonies capable of sustained artificial gravity and easily replicated components. Dr. Jacob Baptista explained the rationale behind the AS investment, stating, "We [GEMI] needed to develop gravity-generating colonies to give us a shot at long-term living and working in space, hopefully free of potential gravity-related pathologies. And, we needed a simple ISH and hub design that could be replicated and interchanged relatively easily across colonies — think Model T–like basic ISH and hub units. AS was laser-focused on this. It was a great fit for us."

[2]Existing space colonies generate artificial gravity by spinning along a central hub axis.

[3]Another artificial gravity-generating colony model, the Yuánzhùtǐ was built by the Chinese between 2033 and 2037. The Yuánzhùtǐ was considered a strong potential competitor to the AS/GEMI hub and spoke space colony model and is still operational in the 2050s. However, the ship has been operating at 70% capacity for the last decade

because of faulty rotating gravitation rings, leaving 30% of the colony without gravitational potential.

The Evolution of the Spaceplane

The first time a spaceplane breached the Kármán line[1] was in 1963, when Joseph A. Walker briefly flew a US Air Force X-15 beyond 100 kilometers in altitude and into space. For the next sixty-five years, the prevailing spaceplane model mimicked the first — a compact, hardened, aerodynamic plane launched from a booster rocket for its ascent into low Earth orbit (LEO) and then gliding back to Earth to be reused. As humanity began to explore and build in space, a patchwork of methods was utilized to transport people and material beyond Earth's atmosphere and into LEO. For the first several decades, these primitive spaceplanes, multiple-stage rockets, and, eventually, space elevators were enlisted in this epic (and protracted) effort. However, these solutions were limited to locations capable of rocket launches or, for materials and perishables, one of three elevator sites near the Equator — limitations that temporarily curtailed the growing demand for safer, more available, and less expensive transportation to space.

These obstacles were overcome in 2028, when Radian Aerospace (RA), aided by \$52 billion in GEMI investments, successfully unveiled the Cricket, the first commercially viable single-stage-to-orbit (SSTO) spaceplane[2] capable of sled-assisted[3] take-off and landing at most airports. In the 2043 PBS documentary, "Space Exploration Milestones," Dr. Jacob Baptista discussed the rationale and economics behind such a steep investment ($233 billion adjusted to 2055 dollars) in an unproven technology.

"We needed the SSTO spaceplane developed. Without it, space exploration and colonization would have remained slow and unavailable to most people," Dr. Baptista said. "We needed a mode of transportation to space within the grasp of everyone — like airplanes and local airports are for Earth travel. Radian had a smart mechanical solution to get this done. They aligned well with our mission, and they had a lot of smart, experienced space industry people behind it."

Retired General Steve Wilson, former US Air Force vice chief and founder of AFWERX, concurred. "Radian is developing one of the most important space vehicles I've seen to date," he said. "Building a responsive, single stage-to-orbit space vehicle that can take off and land from existing runway infrastructure is a game-changer."

Dr. Baptista mused, "Was the cost exorbitant? Maybe. But sometimes, the commitment must be made to get something done — almost regardless of the cost. Look, the Moon landing of the 1960s cost the United States around $800 billion in today's dollars. Was it worth it? Hell, yes. And what about Ti'son Asteroids Corporation[4]? A few years ago, the owner and her investors threw over a trillion dollars into whatever it took to mine asteroids. I read stats a few months ago estimating Ti'son now supplies 90% of the raw material for space colony development and nearly all colony water and mineral needs. Ti'son's revenues are off the charts."

In 2034, Reaction Engines (RE), an Airbus subsidiary, finally succeeded in commercializing its long-awaited SABRE engine[5] technologies. Coupled with aircraft materials advances — most notably graphene-based hull sheathing and engine housing — the RE Skylon SSTO spaceplane made its maiden commercial launch on June 2, 2034, unassisted (i.e., no sled), from the Dallas Fort Worth airport. The Skylon returned to the same airport after shuttling six passengers to one of the Axiom Space Corporation (AS) space hotels, followed by space maneuverability testing, and then gliding back to Earth with three returning AS employees twenty-seven hours later. By the early

2040s, most airlines with space transportation divisions had versions of the SABRE jet engine powering their fleets of spaceplanes, slowly supplanting the pioneering RA sled-assisted model.

More recently, the 2047 introduction of the Boeing StarTec spaceplane heralded a new hybrid class of aircraft able to execute both Earth-bound and space-bound flights. The use of an extremely strong, lightweight graphene-infused sheathing reduced the plane's gross weight by 28%. Coupled with engine power enhancements, the model allowed for true SSTO capability without a specialized engine. Boeing Vice President Kimberly Alberg lauded the ease with which she now occasionally commutes between Earth and Boeing's space colony in medium Earth orbit (MEO), stating, "I can get to our company's colony, 482 miles up, in less than an hour. A 30-minute flight, docking, and I'm in my office looking back at Earth before you know it."

According to the 2050 issue of *Forbes* magazine's "Annual Space Business Opportunities Summary," spaceplanes ferry 96% of people to and from space. Will this trend continue? The Space Investment Group, in their 2051 report, "The State of Near-Earth Space Colonization," stated they believe so: "We have witnessed an increase in spaceplane flights to low- and medium-Earth orbits of over 30% year-over-year for the last decade, with no indication of slowing down. But we consider these numbers misleading because a limiting factor has been — and still is — the lack of available colonies and space stations for travelers, workers, and residents. We don't know when or if this exodus to space will end. The demand is just that great."

Spaceplane technologies will almost certainly continue to evolve into the 2060s, although they will likely focus more on adding spaceship-like capabilities as their routes take them further from Earth. Still, their primary mission is to shuttle people from Earth to LEO and MEO safely. As the space ecosystem grows, spaceplane utilization will continue to grow with it.

———————————

[1] The Fédération Aéronautique Internationale (FAI) defines the Kármán line as space beginning 100 kilometers (54 nautical miles, 62 miles, 330,000 feet) above Earth's mean sea level (Wikipedia, 2040).

[2] A spaceplane model that can launch from an airport runway and still have enough power to reach LEO orbit. Once docked at an established space portal, passengers and cargo are discharged/loaded. The spaceplane then does a controlled glide back to Earth, landing at a designated airport runway like a traditional airplane.

[3] The Radian Aerospace (RA) Cricket spaceplane utilized a modified HyperLoop frictionless rail system to launch from an elongated airport runway, removing the need to expend valuable fuel during the initial take-off (Radian Aerospace product description, 2027).

[4] Lam Ti'son and her investment group, the Ti'son Group, eventually invested more than $1 trillion over a ten-year period in the space asteroid mining industry, which at the time was an unheard-of capital investment in a single high-risk space project. Indeed, shortly after the investment announcement in 2034, the *Wall Street Journal* called the Ti'son Group investment "the most frivolous mega-investment in space we have witnessed to date — one whose possible failure would do nothing to help establish an industrial presence in space." In 2047, Ti'son Asteroids Corporation (TAC) went public, and Lam Ti'son, as majority owner, was recognized as the probable richest person in the solar system, recognizing the nebulous accounting irregularities between the economics of Earth and space colonies.

[5] The SABRE (Synergetic Air-Breathing Rocket Engine) is a new class of air-breathing rocket engine that can propel an aircraft from zero to five times the speed of sound in the atmosphere and twenty-five times the speed of sound for space access (Reaction Engine product description, 2035).

Baptista's \$252 Billion Graphene Gamble

2031

Since its discovery in 2004, graphene (an allotrope of carbon) was considered the only known material strong enough to act as the tether for the then theoretical space elevator transport system. Nevertheless, through the mid-2020s, no research group or company could create more than a few centimeters of graphene string — nowhere near the 150,000 miles of reinforced graphene cabling needed. This changed when, between 2025 and 2030, GEMI spent an unprecedented \$53 billion to develop the means to mass-produce the reinforced graphene necessary to create the cabling needed to bring the space elevator into existence.

For Dr. Baptista, developing a space elevator was essential to GEMI's space goals, and he had a team working on the project within months of GEMI's founding. By the time the space elevator project was announced in 2026, Dr. Baptista had already secured a location for the Earth-bound elevator base and leased a portion of the International Space Station (ISS) for space work related to the project. Dr. Baptista's space elevator team began the construction of the Earth-bound anchor and platform in 2027. At the same time, they began working with SpaceX on rocket cargo missions transporting the necessary material and equipment to the ISS and further into high Earth orbit (stored in orbiting satellite storage units) in preparation for the assembly of the space anchor and spaceport.

By late 2029, between this work and the ongoing graphene R&D, GEMI had spent $105 billion but still had no tether system to show for the investment. When Baptista was asked by a reporter for *The Economist* how he could justify such a capital outlay with possibly no return, Dr. Baptista replied, "It's all about the graphene. We had to develop graphene, or something with similar properties. Without it, there can be no elevator. The cost? When we figure out how to manufacture graphene cabling and sheathing — and we're getting close now — it will more than pay for the initial investment. Just think of the space-based applications for pliable, paper-thin sheets 200 times stronger than steel, eventually made from materials readily available and manufactured in space — and no transportation costs from Earth. Structural sheathing for spaceships, ISHs and hubs, Moon, and Mars colonies. Trust me, it's worth the investment."

True to Dr. Baptista's word, in June of 2030, GEMI researchers aboard the ISS-GEMI finally created a viable manufacturing process for reinforced graphene cabling. This pioneering space-based manufacturing facility utilized large, specialized 3-D printer systems. All material was transported from Earth (space mining for the necessary carbon and hydrogen would not be commercialized until 2037). This graphene manufacturing breakthrough gave Dr. Baptista the green light to finalize the construction of the Earth-bound platform and systems, as well as the space portal, counterbalance, and spaceport, in high Earth orbit. In doing so, GEMI also established the first human-crewed space station in geosynchronous orbit.

This construction work was finalized within the next two years, roughly coinciding with the first 75,000 miles of reinforced graphene manufactured. Project engineers estimated it would take another ten months to manufacture the remaining 72,000 miles needed. The GEMI team used this time to transport the already manufactured cable up to the spaceport location and begin preparations for stringing the cabling down to Earth and launching the space elevator. It would take another two years to successfully lower the cabling over 36,000 miles and attach to the Earth-bound anchor. After another six months of testing, the

GEMI space elevator began operations on June 13, 2035. All told, this Earth- and space-based construction work added another $147 billion to the space elevator system cost, bringing the total cost to build the world's first space elevator to $252 billion.

First Humans on Mars

2031

The five-person crew landed the Martian lander, Collective, on December 9, 2031, at 20:17 UTC (Coordinated Universal Time). Commander Nhung Tran stepped onto the surface of Mars six hours and thirty-nine minutes later, on December 10, 2031, at 02:56 UTC. As with the first manned moon mission sixty-two years earlier, their first step on the surface of Mars reverberated within the global community. The lander pilot, Dr. Maja Svensson, along with engineers Billy Jiang and Tania Chandra and physician Alika Usman, then joined Tran on Mars to begin what amounted to a fast-paced, three-month construction project along the northeastern border of Arcadia Planitia[1] in the northern hemisphere. The sixth team member, Dr. Doris Li, remained on Sky Rover (SR)[2], the extended-stay support ship. Commander Tran and their team of five internationally selected astronauts[3] had committed to spending over one and a half years in space, facing dangers never experienced before, and — with an average distance of 142 million miles between Mars and Earth — no safety net.

The trip to Mars took 209 days. On December 4, 2031, the long-haul spacecraft, Primus[4], entered Mars orbit and, two days later, docked with SR. All six team members transferred to SR, and a day later, the unmanned Primus landed on Mars for refueling. Two days after the Primus Mars landing, Collective launched from SR, transporting the five crew members to the surface of Mars and into the history books. When the mission was completed, Dr. Li used the Cricket

Mars Lander[5] to join the others on the surface, and Primus successfully returned the six astronauts back to Earth.

The SR, controlled remotely by Earth-bound engineers, had been in Mars's orbit for eleven months already, executing numerous tasks in preparation for the arrival of Primus. The ship finalized the exact landing sites for Collective and Primus and analyzed local weather patterns to optimize the timing of the historic manned landing. In addition, SR performed a series of capture-launch-landings of fourteen large cargo satellites near the target landing site. These cargo containers[6] were placed into Mars orbit during five previous missions launched from Earth over the prior four years. The containers were loaded with scientific equipment, two rover vehicles, a small backhoe, construction materials and tools, fuel components, and consumables to be utilized during the upcoming mission.

The astronauts spent 119 days on the surface of Mars. During this time, they recycled several of the cargo containers to build a cluster of six interconnected, special-purpose domes for their use and for future missions. They reinforced three dome habitats they would live and work in with thick, tarp-like sheets tightly woven with boron nitride nanotubes (BNNTs) threading[7] — then the best solution for partial Galactic Cosmic Radiation (GCR) shielding. They stabilized and added additional capacity to the existing twin in-situ oxygen and fuel CO_2 collector/converters, as well as potable water harvesting and purifier systems. They also surveyed and marked the perimeters of two large, stable, flat regions near their colony site to use for future ship landings and launches.

This mission was funded, developed, and executed by a consortium that included Lockheed Martin, SpaceX, GEMI, Blue Origin, Relativity Space, Impulse Space, MIT, Stanford, and other companies, universities, numerous countries, and investor groups — but notably was not government-sponsored. Indeed, many economists consider this mission the turning point for the reduction of government-sponsored space missions. NASA, CNSA, ISRO, RSA, and other government space agencies began significantly downsizing their space programs in the 2030s, relying instead on the fast-moving private sector to develop the critically important space ecosystem.

Together, the consortium spent over $58 billion on the mission. The cost was especially steep because the goals of the mission differed from earlier science-based missions, demanding more development of technologies focused on colonization — not "just" landing people on Mars. GEMI Chief Scientist Dr. Jacob Baptista explained, "We [the consortium] were roundly criticized for our aggressive agenda for this trip. We put a premium on safety, of course, but, hey, we were traveling fourteen months and about 400 million miles — we were not going to just plant a flag on Mars and collect Mars rock samples. We needed to be bold in not only getting to Mars, but also in preparing for the next steps in colonization. We're building a viable, permanent colony on Mars, and this mission was Phase I."

There have been dozens of trips to Mars in the quarter century since the historic first manned mission. While we have essentially routinized travel to and habitation on Mars, we continue to be fascinated with and drawn to the red planet. Business ventures, scientific research, mining operations, a launching point for ever deeper space exploration, and even tourism — all contribute to our increasing colonization of Mars. As we continue to push further into space, the first manned Mars landing and the fledgling colony established will continue to stand as important milestones in space exploration.

-----

[1]This sector in the northern hemisphere of Mars has been one of the focus regions for colony development since this first manned landing. With the advent of graphene sheathing and cosmic radiation shielding, the plains of Arcadia Planitia have become a thriving multi-national hive of domes and utility buildings. The International Space Census (ISC) agency estimated that in 2055, there were approximately 7,000 people living and working in the three colony clusters on the plains of Arcadia Planitia. In addition to these colony communities, there are also numerous small scientific colonies and mining exploratory parties scattered around the planet.

[2]Similar in concept to the earlier International Space Station (ISS), SR is a modular orbiting vehicle designed to orbit Mars as the local support center for multi-national missions to Mars. SR is still orbiting Mars, although now relegated to the role of an off-planet hospital.

[3]The UN facilitated an exhaustive, unbiased, and transparent international search for the thirty astronauts who participated in the first manned mission to Mars. That no one from the G20 countries was selected was — to many — surprising, refreshing, and reassuring. An excerpt from a *Wall Street Journal* opinion piece on the successful mission commented, "Those chosen for the first manned mission to Mars reaffirm that we are all valued humans capable of anything we're willing to work hard for."

[4]In 2030, SpaceX introduced the company's latest long-haul, reusable Starship model, Starship III. The Starship Primus was, at the time, the most powerful rocket ever made.

[5]A reusable minimalist lander capable of soft landing of no more than two astronauts on the surface. If refueling is available, the lander can be reused.

[6]Cargo satellites have been used extensively since the late 2020s to support missions to the Moon, Mars, and other destinations. Loaded with supplies needed for upcoming missions, these containers are typically placed into a low orbit (sometimes years in advance) to later be landed on the target surface. Often, these same containers are "recycled" as surface habitats, reducing the weight and space needed on starships and saving thousands of hours of construction time.

[7]A polymorph of boron nitride that can withstand high temperatures of up to 900 °C and are capable of absorbing radiation (Wikipedia, 2027).

Families in Space

2030 – 2055

The proliferation of novel colonies in near- and mid-Earth orbits through the late 2030s enticed the first few pioneering families to space. Still, it was not until galactic cosmic radiation[1] shielding was patented by GEMI scientists in 2036 that people and their families began to flock to deep space. This material essentially removed the threat of radiation poisoning and cancer from unshielded exposure to space radiation. Commercialized in licensing partnership with space materials giant ESI[2] in 2038, this shielding literally caused a spike in the birthrate in space. Once this last tangible danger to living in deep space was eliminated, colonies and corporations began expanding outward, with more and more family units signing on for longer, more permanent space-based assignments.

The first documented relationship between two people in space occurred a month into the first manned mission to Mars in late 2031. Two engineers, Dr. Tania Chandra and Billy Jiang, announced their engagement during an onboard team meeting. Tania and Billy made history again when they were married the following June during the return trip to Earth, with the ship's commander, Nhong Tran, officiating. In an interview with the *New York Times*, Dr. Chandra explained their motivation for getting married in space. "We were aware we were the first to get married in space, but this choice was for us — not a headline," she said. "We met during our two years of training for this mission, and we fell in love. It just seemed like a fun way to start our lives together."

While the first marriage in space was unique, the first "space baby" shook the world, polarizing those for or against family-friendly space colonization. Alya (a Hebrew name meaning "ascend") was born by Cesarean section in the small near-Earth Chevron research colony, spinning at 28,000 km/hour, 520 kilometers above Earth, at 17:36 UTC on June 4, 2034. She weighed 3.2 kg and was 53 cm long. Her birth parents were Dr. Noa Peretz, MD, the colony general physician, and her husband, Dr. Ariel Peretz, an energy engineer. When asked by *Family* magazine if she was apprehensive about birthing her baby in space, Dr. Peretz explained, "We had lots of support from Chevron — they were even prepared to fly us back to Earth quickly if there were any complications. But I had total confidence in the procedure and that Alya would be safe, and she was. And yes, we plan to continue living in the colony. I know the science. It's safe, as long as we stay in close orbit to Earth."

Deciding whether to birth and raise children in space was a commitment unlike most Earth-bound parents would ever need to contemplate, especially since most scientists and medical professionals at the time recommended that a child born in space should stay in space. They cited a litany of actual and potential biological, psychological, and skeletal challenges that may impact a space-born child on Earth. But the science did not deter everyone. Indeed, the first decennial International Space Census (ISC), published in 2041, reported that within the existing 221 colonies, eighty-three children were born in space between 2034 and 2040. The recently published 2050 ISC census reported that this number had climbed to 3,707 babies born in space across the 2,433 registered colonies between 2040 and 2050.

In an interview with the *Wall Street Journal* shortly after Alya's birth, Dr. Duarte discussed the significance of this historic first baby born in space. "We didn't really think about families in space before Alya, but you could almost feel attitudes shifting once families became part of the picture," she said. "Suddenly, colony-based healthcare, sustenance, safety, and financial security, combined with the question of how to ascribe the nationality of a child born in space, all became that much more important. Even governments were quick to enact policies surrounding the nationalities of children and families — I don't know, maybe trying to control human space expansion? Good luck with that. In any case, we've definitely entered a new chapter in space with Alya's birth. Oh, and by the way, her mother, Nuria, is a GEMI alum — she's a real Martian!"

Author's note: As of 2055, there have been no discernible differences in health-related metrics between children born and raised in space compared to Earth children.

Tania and Billy have been happily married for 23 years. Alya, now 21 years old, is an internist with Hubbard Asteroid Mining. She lives, studies, and works in the Hubbard L4 Space Colony — a sprawling work and research colony on the edge of the Jupiter trojan asteroid swarm. Alya has made two short visits to Earth.

Alya's mother created tension between Earth-based governments and space colonies when she refused to recognize Israel as Alya's nation of origin on her birth certificate, allowing only Chevron Space Research Colony to be noted on the document. While the Israeli government still registered Alya as a sovereign citizen of Israel, this space-based resistance to Earth-bound authority sparked international debates that have continued into the 2050s.

---

[1]Heavy, high-energy ions of elements that have had all their electrons stripped away as they journeyed through the galaxy at nearly the speed of light. They can cause atoms they pass through to ionize, and they can pass nearly unimpeded through a typical spacecraft or the skin of an astronaut (NASA, 2033).

[2]ESI is the largest space-based corporation in existence. Revenues from 2055 were estimated at $83 trillion U.S. (Economics Media, 2056).

GEMI Space Elevator Goes into Operation

The GEMI space elevator began operations on June 13, 2035, instantly becoming a wonder of the world. More than any other previous milestone met, this successful deployment of the space elevator put GEMI in the world spotlight, demonstrating the enormous capability of the GEMI brain trust and capital. Dr. Hana Duarte described witnessing the historic first lift, stating, "They put us in the bunker-like control complex — safer, I guess. From where we stood, I could see the massive anchoring loop embedded deep in the island bedrock, and the tethers arched up from the anchor into the sky until they just faded away. The island was low and flat and mostly covered by the steel and concrete EarthPort that reminded me of an aircraft carrier deck. Then the countdown, and swish — the lifter shot up and, I don't know, maybe thirty seconds later, disappeared. An amazing sight! I was so proud of the GEMI team."

The historic first payload weighed 1,312 kilos, and the manifest listed aluminum framing, foodstuff, and a case of champagne (to celebrate the event) to be delivered to the endpoint GEO SpacePort and its crew 22,000 miles up. This was the first of thousands of shipments that have made up the docket for the elevator since then. Indeed, by the time the elevator was operational, there were already over 600 certified payload orders (reviewed, approved, and scheduled by GEMI) and thousands of orders still awaiting analysis and scheduling — which, considering the elevator cost roughly $250 billion to build, was good news for GEMI. Through the 2030s, using rocket-based transportation to launch and place an object into orbit cost upwards of $3,000/kg. In contrast, the GEMI space elevator could handle as many as five lifter-loads per day of up to 22,000 kg per lifter, at an average cost of only $340/kg — thus creating the first "disruptor" within the space transport industry and a huge demand for the elevator.

Anchored in the bedrock of an isolated South Pacific island on the equator, multiple reinforced graphene cables rise 36,000 miles to a 15,000-ton counterbalance platform located 14,000 miles beyond geo-synchronous orbit (GEO). The elevator tether passes through four spaceport platforms on the way to the endpoint GEO SpacePort. These four platforms are roughly equidistant through low Earth orbit (LEO) and medium Earth orbit (MEO). At their destination platform, cargo is launched through a transfer orbit (TO) into a predetermined orbit based on the payload's purpose. Highly automated, the elevator cargo "lifter" usually spends an hour or so at each spaceport waystation while automatons remove each designated satellite/container and launch it (akin to firing from a cannon) through a TO to its designated orbit.

At any given time, there are up to ten lifters on the elevator tether system: five ascending and five descending. They are spaced roughly 5,000 miles apart along the tether. Once a lifter has delivered its pay-load(s) to one or more spaceports, it will transfer to the descending tether system to return to the EarthPort and receive another shipment. Lifter speeds range from 500 miles per hour to over 1,000 miles per hour as they move up and down the tether — a lifter traveling non-stop would take approximately 26 hours to reach the SpacePort at GEO. However, most lifters deposit their cargo at one or more of the four intermediate spaceports and then transfer to the descending tether system for the trip back to Earth.

By the time the historic GEMI space elevator went operational, GEMI and other corporations were already discussing opportunities with potential partners to build additional space elevators. Within five years, two more elevators were built — one off the western coast of

Africa and one off the eastern coast of South America — and in 2049, a fourth elevator was constructed on a small atoll in the southern Maldives.

Most analysts agree that four space elevators are sufficient, even with the dramatic increase in space travel, colonization, and commerce the world has witnessed in the last decade. A graphene industry analyst with *The Economist* stated in 2051, "The use of space planes to routinely transport supplies, in addition to people to space, has been one factor in leveling the demand for elevator cargo space. Another is the expansion of the space-based graphene industry mining and manufacturing operations during the same period. While there will be, for the foreseeable future, a strong elevator demand for technologies and sustenance from Earth, the growing availability of space-based supplies of graphene-derived materials for building structures in space has slowly reduced the elevator backlog. However, across the four elevators, the average backlog is still nearly seven months, consisting mostly of foodstuff and advanced technologies not yet economically manufactured in space."

International Outer Space Treaty Ratified

2037

After the successful Russian Sputnik 1 satellite launch in 1957, world leaders recognized and acted on the need to regulate future outer space explorations. By December of the following year, the United Nations General Assembly adopted its first outer space resolution, "Question of the peaceful use of outer space." In 1961, U.S. President John F. Kennedy said in his address to the UN General Assembly, "As we extend the rule of law on earth, so must we also extend it to man's new domain — outer space." By 1967, the UN General Assembly established the first outer space treaty, the Treaty on Principles Governing the Activities of States in the Exploration and Use of Outer Space, including the Moon and Other Celestial Bodies. Also known as the "Magna Carta of Space," by 1984, this broad agreement was followed by four other resolutions collectively called the "Outer Space Treaty."

These forward-looking international agreements were somewhat surprising as space exploration was still in its infancy, with the Apollo 11 mission's Moon landing still two years in the future. While 157 countries eventually signed most of these resolutions, it was not until 2037, more than fifty years after the creation of the original Outer Space Treaty, that an updated, more comprehensive set of resolutions called the International Outer Space Treaty (IOST) was ratified and adopted by more than 200 countries. By this time, an estimated 20,000 artificial objects were orbiting the Earth, thousands of people were living and working in space, and private companies were initiating more and larger projects. A 2035 *Astronomy* magazine special commemorative report, "The State of Space Exploration," stated, "To date, outer space scientific and commercial missions have taken humankind to five planets, eleven moons, and dozens of asteroids within our solar system. Roughly three-quarters of these missions were privately funded." World leaders, rightly so, were worried they were losing control of the space frontier.

Yang Sying, the China National Space Administration (CNSA) Administrator in 2038, explained, "You have commercial space planes making several trips to low orbit space daily, shuttling hundreds of people to and from space transportation hubs. The GEMI space elevator has been operating twenty-four hours a day and is backlogged for almost two years. There are nearly 200 space colonies orbiting the Earth and dozens of deep space mining explorations underway. But this is only the beginning. How are we going to control all this? We are not. Countries were not invited to the party. It is not like the American Gold Rush, when the United States at least owned the land and was able to wrest control of the regions as they were settled. We are not going to have that option in space. It is unsettling, but it is reality."

One of the critical challenges in developing a realistic set of articles in the treaty was the need to allow enough flexibility in the regulations so as not to hinder the ability of private (non-governmental) companies to make a profit from space enterprises. From the early 2000s, government leaders encouraged the ongoing contributions of private companies in space transportation, exploration, and living and working in space. In fact, by 2035, nearly 100% of space-related government projects were executed through partnerships with private companies. As a result, most countries scaled back their space initiatives, relying instead on the growing expertise and commercial systems available in the private sector.

Below are a few salient new or updated items ratified within the 2037 International Outer Space Treaty (IOST):

- Modeled after the long-standing global air-traffic management (GATM) system implemented through the United Nations-based agency International Civil Aviation Organization (ICAO), the treaty mandated the development of the Space Object Management System (SOMS). Completed in 2043, SOMS monitors natural objects (mostly small asteroids) and artificial objects (satellites, space planes and ships, colony clusters, elevator cabling systems, platforms, space shuttle buses, and space junk) in low- to mid-Earth orbit and manages the air space from 100 km to 40,000 km above the Earth's surface.

- Space elevator cabling systems extend from the Earth's surface to the point in space allowing geosynchronous orbit — 35,786 km (22,236) miles high. While most of the cabling and platforms would disintegrate on re-entry to Earth, the 50-60 miles of cabling system closest to Earth could cause devastating damage along its path of entry. Any country or corporation planning to build a space elevator must adhere to exacting construction specifications and geo-spacing restrictions to ensure the safety of the regions surrounding the proposed elevator site location.

- The existing ban on space-based weapons was more clearly articulated to include technologies not previously in existence.

- Recognizing the fluidity of the space exodus, the IOST board will schedule annual meetings to review, modify, and/or add treaty components.

- Ownership and purpose by entities in outer space must be registered with IOST, including:
    - Colonies funded, built, or purchased.
    - Registered ships, ISHs, hubs, stations, or other structures constructed or purchased either on Earth or in outer space.
    - Structures (above and below the surface) on celestial objects (moons, asteroids, and planets) and domain over land extending beyond the structure (dependent on the size of the celestial object).

- Policy development and ongoing operational costs of the IOST and SOMS will be assumed by all involved parties, including countries, corporations, and educational institutions.

Many countries with established space programs strongly opposed this new model, notably the United States, India, and China. India's Prime Minister, Raj Shah, summarized their position early in the treaty process: "Putting corporations on an equal footing with countries is a recipe for disaster. A coalition of sovereign countries should control the development and enforcement of the laws governing human progression into outer space."

However, outer space's rich, untapped economic potential, combined with the overwhelming majority of relevant intellectual property and technologies owned by private corporations, proved to be the tipping points. Even these world powers eventually consented and ratified the treaty.

Space Traffic and Debris Control: Monitoring and Management

2042

Through the 2020s, Earth-to-space flights were still relatively infrequent. However, by 2025, the number of pieces of orbital space debris had already reached roughly 30,000 objects, with NASA predictions reaching up to 50,000 by 2050. In 2032, Dr. Nils Moe, the Director General of the European Space Agency (ESA), described the growing urgency to create a space-based traffic management system. "It is getting quite hairy up there – especially in lower Earth orbits. We [space agencies and private companies] have been pushing satellites into higher orbits for a while now. However, there are still roughly 7,000 active satellites in low Earth orbit (LEO). Add to that number maybe 35,000 space debris objects, flying at 20,000-plus miles per hour, most of which are capable of damaging a spacecraft, and you have an increased potential for a catastrophic accident in space. Even at just a few centimeters in size, it does not take much mass at that speed to do damage," Moe said.

By 2035, the number of space debris[1] objects reached 38,000, and the need to carefully monitor and manage all functional and non-functional, human-made, and natural space traffic had become critical. While numerous governmental space agencies had developed early, basic systems to inventory and track space debris, in 2037, the newly ratified International Outer Space Treaty (IOST) mandated the development of "…an autonomous system capable of the real-time tracking and managing of natural and artificial objects orbiting or otherwise moving through low- to mid-Earth space." The Space Object Management System (SOMS) aided companies such as ClearSpace[2] and SpaceServices[3] in tackling the space debris problem. By 2055, the number of pieces of space debris dropped to approximately 18,000, with an estimated yearly reduction of 5-10% projected through 2060. In contrast, within the same time frame, SOMS reported the number of natural and non-debris artificial objects in near-Earth orbits at any time exceeded 25,000 objects, including an average of one hundred daily flights from Earth (mostly spaceplanes).

---

[1]Defunct human-made objects in space, principally in Earth orbit, which no longer serve a useful function (Wikipedia contributors, September 2032).

[2]Founded in 2018 and one of the pioneering service-oriented space companies, ClearSpace focuses on retrieving space debris and artificial objects deemed reusable (if captured). ClearSpace successfully retrieved its first object in 2025.

[3]Founded in 2026, SpaceServices is a catch-all space shuttle service with numerous offerings, including space debris retrieval and ferrying services between colonies.

Space Tourism

2025 – 2055

In the last century, tourism on Earth has significantly grown in popularity. Naturally, as space travel became more accessible, less expensive, and safer, tourists were quick to look to space for their next adventure. Indeed, space tourism was an early driver of Earth-to-space transportation and space colony development. In the unregulated space ecosystem of the late-2020s through the mid-2030s, roughly 50% of the handful of low-Earth orbit (LEO) colonies constructed, and 60% of spaceplane flights reserved, were primarily for space tourism. Investors were following the money.

Nonetheless, space tourism was slow to gain traction until spaceplanes were routinized and enough colony real estate was available to house and entertain space tourists. The first space tourist was transported to the International Space Station (ISS) on a Russian Soyuz rocket on April 30, 2001. Dennis Tito, an American millionaire, paid $20 million to fulfill a lifetime dream to go to space — and secure his footnote in space history. Still, by 2020, only two dozen non-professional astronauts had joined ranks with Tito, mainly through arrangements (and payments) with Russian or U.S. space programs. Fast forward to 2055: More than 4.7 million tourists have made at least one trip to space.

Pioneer entrepreneurs in the commercial space industry, Elon Musk (SpaceX), Sir Richard Branson (Virgin Galactic), and Jeff Bezos (Blue Origin) all recognized this emerging market opportunity. Equipped with early vertical-flight, multiple-stage spaceplanes and rockets, they aggressively pursued the space tourism businesses, catering to the few wealthy clientele[1] willing to pay for the experience of traveling on a sub-orbital spaceflight[2]. Then, in 2028 came the introduction of single-stage-to-orbit (SSTO) spaceplanes, capable of taking off and landing on most commercial airport runways. It was then that space tourism had the wings — and the requisite volume — to take off as an industry.

SSTO spaceplanes were vital. When Radian Aerospace Corp. (RA) commercialized its Cricket SSTO spaceplane in 2028, traditional airlines were quick to leverage their airline industry expertise with the mass space transportation opportunities this technology presented. They invested in further developing SSTO spaceplanes, Earth-to-LEO flight corridor satellites, and hybrid spaceports/hotels, adding this new market to their existing Earth-bound airline industry. At the same time, airports around the world hurried to equip one or more runways to accommodate spaceplane specifications. Evolving through the 2030s, commercial spaceplanes were routinized in the 2040s, and by the early 2050s, thousands of passengers were shuttled to commercial LEO and MEO spaceports daily for both work and leisure.

Addressing the need for lodging and entertainment for these early space tourists, the space construction company Pinnacle built and opened the first space hotel, the Pinnacle Space Station (PSS), in the summer of 2029. While PSS did not have artificial gravity[3], within two years of the successful Pinnacle opening, three more space hotels were constructed in LEO and began operations. All three were funded by collaborations among numerous Earth-bound airlines, speculative private investor groups, and hotel moguls. These sprawling space superstructures were a mix of leisure hotels and commercial work and research hubs.

Into the mid-2050s, the space hotel market is still accelerating. Now numbering approximately 300, these space hotels have grown into elaborate space colonies, some with hundreds of hubs and thousands of ISHs used for residential living, work, research, and tourism. In addition to LEO and MEO orbits, space colonies can now be found on the Moon, Mars, numerous asteroids, Titan (Saturn's largest moon), and within the Earth-Moon Lagrange Points[4] L4 and L5. From these still exotic destinations, tourists participate in activities ranging from simple sightseeing to exploring planets and moons, and even asteroid mining.

Will the space tourism industry continue to see triple-digit growth beyond the 2050s? A November 2054 *Wall Street Journal* opinion piece titled "A Space Tourism Bubble?" mused, "Is space tourism going to fade away? We reference the still long lines of adventure tourists on Mount Everest every year in our argument that interest in space tourism will only increase. This year, more than a hundred space flights are available from dozens of airports worldwide each day, and there are over 300 destination space stations to choose from for a few days of lodging — many for under $50,000. Unfortunately, there are also months-long waiting lists for each, and we believe we are still at least a decade away from meeting market demand.

"For the year 2055, Statista reported worldwide Earth-bound tourism receipts of nearly $23 trillion (9.1% of global GDP). In the same report, space tourism accounted for 29% of gross revenue generated within space-based economies. While we cannot expect this boom to continue indefinitely, space tourism will factor heavily in space-based economies for the foreseeable future."

Author's note: Already an airline business veteran, Branson and his Virgin Galactic company adjusted as spaceplanes were commercialized and still competes successfully in the space airline business. SpaceX and Blue Origin pivoted their space businesses into other lucrative, non-spaceplane enterprises.

---

[1]Unlike today's $7,000 tickets to one of the dozens of commercial LEO spaceports, in the 2020s, only professional astronauts and the very wealthy had the resources to travel to space. Space tourists during that period paid anywhere from $100,000 for a short duration sub-orbital flight to up to $55 million (2020 figures) for a multi-day mission to the *only* space destination existing at the time — the International Space Station (ISS).

[2]A spaceflight in which the spacecraft reaches outer space, but its trajectory intersects the atmosphere or surface of the gravitating body from which it was launched, so that it will not complete one orbital revolution (it does not become an artificial satellite) or reach escape velocity (Wikipedia, 2033).

[3]The first few space hotels and stations did not have artificial gravity capabilities and were used for relatively short work and tourism excursions. The first *commercial artificial gravity* space station was the Delta Spaceport, a joint venture by Axiom Space (AS), GEMI, and private investors, christened in early 2033.

[4]Positions in space where objects sent there tend to stay put. At Lagrange Points, the gravitational pull of two large masses precisely equals the centripetal force required for a small object to move with them. These points in space are used by spacecraft to reduce the fuel consumption needed to remain in position (NASA, 2031).

Space Gold Rush

2040 – 2055

In 2017, the now-defunct World Economic Forum (WEF) observed, "Companies around the world — in transportation, exploration, energy, construction, or hospitality — are all looking upwards for the next growth opportunity. Space is quickly becoming a place where the industries that power our global economy will conduct business."

It took some time, but by 2040, what most contemporary economists call the Space Gold Rush began in earnest. By then, two additional higher-capacity space elevators were in operation, more than quadrupling the capacity to quickly and inexpensively transport the construction materials, technologies, and consumables needed in space. As well, the success of the first few artificial gravity space colonies, and the commercialization of the incredibly strong graphene-infused sheathing used in space hulls and shielding, gave people the confidence that they could safely live, work, and vacation in space for extended periods. Finally, advances in single-stage-to-orbit (SSTO) spaceplanes brought affordable and widely available transportation to the tens of thousands of people from around the world needing or wanting to travel to space.

Serendipitously, worldwide, the larger infrastructure-related urban construction megaprojects initiated in the 2020s to reduce emissions of CO_2, were beginning to wind down, culminating in the dissolution of IMPF in the late 2040s and freeing up trillions of dollars in investment capital. As a sustainable space ecosystem quickly evolved, this capital further fueled an investment frenzy in space that has continued to accelerate, with no end in sight into the mid-2050s.

The International Monetary Fund (IMF) stated in their 2054 annual *Space Economies Forecast Report*, "For the foreseeable future, the need for space habitats will far exceed availability. This intense demand has, incredibly, accelerated in the last few years — and not for lack of investment capital. During the 2040s, we witnessed $34 trillion pour into space-related enterprises and colony development. Nearly halfway through the 2050s, investors have already committed an additional $26 trillion in space, so we might very well see total space investments in excess of $50 trillion (2054 dollars) by the end of the decade."

Certainly, halfway through the 2050s, there is still a fascination with and a pent-up demand for everything space. Even with four space elevators, true SSTO spaceplanes, and substantial investment capital, colony developers are struggling to satisfy their investors and customers as they vie to obtain the material and technologies they need to continue building colonies. Despite these Earth/space supply chain challenges, in only two decades, the number of colonies has grown from just several dozen small, primarily single-hub outposts to over 2,500 robust colony communities, ranging up to sprawling colonies with dozens of hubs, hundreds of ISHs, and populations in the tens of thousands.

New York Times Chief Economist Dr. Linda McDonald lamented in a 2053 essay, "Most political and business leaders did not see the Space Gold Rush coming, at least not to this extent or this intensity. I confess I also did not. But it's here now — no denying that — and we are racing to understand and adapt to this new business and social environment. As governance and business strategies continue to evolve in this wildly growing, entrepreneurial ecosystem literally not of this world, a new economic beast is emerging."

Some larger sectors, such as space tourism, transportation to and from space, and construction of orbiting, lunar, and other planetary habitats, have already been building their markets for as long as three decades. According to IMF, space tourism alone, a growth industry since the mid-2020s, now accounts for fully 30% of all Earth-based revenue generated by space-facing businesses in 2055. In addition, the 2054 *Space Airlines Industry Annual Report* noted that 99% of the people traveling to space — 80% of whom are tourists — do so via commercially available spaceplanes. Seventeen airlines with spaceplanes make nearly one hundred regularly scheduled trips beyond the Kármán line daily. While such trips are limited to a maximum of fifty passengers[1] per flight, nearly two million people are expected to travel to space this year, most of whom are destined for hospitality colonies.

While the space transportation and construction industries still have persistent supply chain challenges, specialized businesses are nonetheless rushing to enter this ever-expanding space ecosystem. Into the 2050s, there are now roughly 10,000 businesses dedicated entirely to space-based commerce. Recognizing the scarcity of resources across most space colonies, these businesses supply services ranging from delivering food and other consumables, providing specialized medical attention, and offering local (intra-space) transportation, to larger endeavors such as managing the operations of entire colonies. Such niche space businesses are collectively finding ways to fill resource gaps, contributing to the fledgling space-based economies developing within and across colonies. In the process, these enterprises, according to a 2054 Morgan Stanley analysis, "have carved out space colony markets worth, collectively, $11 trillion in 2053 alone."

In 2055, the space ecosystem is expanding exponentially. However, there are many unknowns surrounding this movement. What additional regulations will Earth-bound governments impose on space businesses, commerce, colonies, and exploration? What does the commitment to building space-based businesses mean for business owners in the long run? What taxes might be levied for businesses incorporated in space? It is too early to answer these and other questions, but with trillion-dollar markets in the offing, regardless of risks, the enormous opportunities in space are too numerous to be ignored by entrepreneurs and investors.

————————————

[1]SSTO spaceplane technical weight limitations restrict the number of passengers per flight. This weight restriction is necessary to successfully break free of Earth's gravitational pull, reach orbital velocity, and cross the Kármán line.

Space Societies and Cultural Development

2055

How might societal structure and cultural norms morph due to long-term living and working in space? What relationships will develop among space colonies and the Earth-bound corporations, investors, and governments that funded them? Space colonization is still in its infancy, allowing only speculation about what societal and cultural differences might manifest in space colonies during the coming years. However, some observations are worth noting.

We are witnessing an extraordinary exodus to space. More than three million people have uprooted their lives on Earth in the last two decades, moving themselves and their families to space colonies. So far, most of this migration has been to low- and medium-Earth orbits (LEOs and MEOs). However, with the commercialization of the lightweight and fast Nuclear Thermal Rocket (NTR)-driven spaceship (developed by NASA in 2041) and the lightweight shielding that protects against almost all space radiation (commercialized by GEMI in 2038), more colonies are now moving further beyond Earth's orbit. While the numbers are still small, colonies are now scattered to the Moon, to within Earth-Moon Lagrange points, to Mars, and to multi-year mining missions in the asteroid belt.

The immense monetary value embedded in the asteroid belt has been known for many decades. Rare metals alone, mined from just a handful of asteroids, would be worth many times the current global

GDP. However, following discoveries of organic material within asteroids in the 2020s, thousands of asteroids with similar profiles have since been identified as having extensive caches of water (ice) and the minerals that make up the building blocks of life.

Tapping into this rich organic resource, especially as space colonization extends further from Earth, can potentially reduce, or eliminate space colony dependence on Earth-based sources for their material and life-support needs. Many cultural anthropologists argue that this freedom will, in turn, foster psychological independence. A June 2051 article in the *Journal of Cultural Anthropology* stated, "The ability to meet their basic material needs, independent of Earth, will pave the way to natural shifts in 'native' space colony-based cultural norms less tainted by Earth-bound cultural influences."

Since the mid-2040s, colonies have engaged in extensive barter-based commerce among themselves. Construction materials, excess foodstuff, medical supplies, and specialized medical services have comprised the predominant trade items. More recently, colony-based digital currency has emerged within the barter economy, although still not yet guaranteed by any central financial institution. Financial analysts are watching these developments, especially as asteroid mining picks up. A March 2053 BlackRock *New Markets* report stated, "Asteroid belt mining — especially for rare metals — while risky, is an enormous opportunity for companies doing business on Earth. Even so, the largest sustainable market may be deep space colonies needing a ready source of water and nutrient-based minerals, known to be in abundance in thousands of identified asteroids. The currency to be used in these transactions is, however, still unclear."

Lastly, representatives from several larger commercial mega-colonies have been present at three recent annual International Space Management Summits (ISMS). They submitted a proposal outlining the rationale and general framework for space colony autonomy during the 2054 summit. Many government delegates voiced concern over even allowing the proposal to be included in the summit minutes. Susan Williams, the U.S. delegate and Acting Assistant Secretary, Office of

Space Affairs, stated, "Earth-bound organizations and governments developed almost all existing space colonies to further our collective interests in space. Logically, we all want to continue to own and protect our substantial investments." The proposal was shelved, but the seeds were planted.

Author's note: I asked Dr. Duarte, a cultural anthropologist herself, in what directions she thought space colony culture might evolve. "It's all still so new. I don't think we're going to see any real cultural differences emerge for another few years," she said. "But still, what we're witnessing in space is unprecedented in human history. Humanity has almost always been on the move, of course, but this is a clean slate with dimensions we have never been exposed to before — especially with deep space colonization. Extreme isolation, minimal 'natural habitat,' the long-term blending of existing cultures. How much Earth-based influence will there be over the long term? No one knows."

Epilogue

2056

The last three decades were a contentious, soul-searching, creative, and ultimately unifying period for humankind. As we traversed the 2020s, we experienced two catastrophic worldwide pandemics and two global terrorist attacks, exposing flaws in participating in tightly interdependent global health, digital, and financial communities. These events, many economists believe, planted the seeds for the regionalism[1] movements still playing out on Earth and in space in the late 2050s. This period also saw the beginning of an increased frequency of extreme weather, presenting us with the stark realities of global warming — and the collective empathy to finally confront it as a global community.

Cleaner, carbon-free, and renewable energy now powers our lives. We have embraced electric transportation, all but eliminating the internal combustion engine and its associated fossil fuel consumption. Most of the world's major cities have implemented new or renovated transportation, power, water, and waste infrastructures. Enforceable international treaties, armed with a satellite system capable of monitoring thousands of pollutants anywhere on Earth, have been established to protect the resources vital to our biosphere. While we will feel the impact of the damage we have wrought on our environment for decades, we are finally on the brink of net zero CO_2 emissions[2].

We are still in our infancy in space, but we are making prodigious strides. Regularly scheduled commercial spaceplanes fly us daily from standard airports to destinations in low-Earth orbit (LEO), enabling us to live, work, and tour across the roughly 2,500 colonies now making up the fledgling space ecosystem. Our equator is home to four space elevators that, together with spaceplanes and conventional rockets, are working around the clock to supply the needs of these colonies and other space enterprises. We have advanced our satellite systems, affording us ubiquitous global communications. As well, asteroid mining and other space-based businesses are beginning to reap the rewards of trillions of dollars in risky investments, fueling even more investment in space exploration and industry. Indeed, the International Monetary Fund (IMF) projects' space-based industries will account for nearly 6% of global (and space) GDP by 2065.

GEMI now includes 106 research and development centers and nearly 15,000 satellite offices worldwide and in space. GEMI has trained millions of young people from nearly every country in the world in one or more scientific disciplines, giving the poorer among us opportunities most would not have had otherwise. GEMI was also a financial boon for the communities around the world fortunate enough to host a GEMI center. GEMI poured billions of dollars into these centers, compounding this infusion through careful management of the multiplier effect. The IMF estimates GEMI, through its first three decades, infused upwards of $30 trillion in these local economies. GEMI also spearheaded many of the period's larger, riskier space projects, supplying both expertise and financial backing. The first space elevator, the SSTO spaceplane, space-based graphene-infused building material, galactic cosmic radiation shielding, and early artificial gravity space colony development — the foundation of the fledgling space ecosystem we are still building in the late-2050s — owe their existence, in large part, to GEMI's deep pockets and Dr. Baptista's vision of space exploration.

At its peak in 2047, IMPF held assets of $76 trillion and was one of the largest corporations in the world. To the surprise of many, that same year, IMPF CEO Patricia Koenigsberg announced that, per corporate bylaws developed by Edward Fisher in the late 2020s, IMPF and all its subsidiaries would be dissolved in the most profitable manner as quickly as possible. They completed the dissolution in 2052 after selling regional segments of the sprawling global business to eighty-seven, carefully selected and locally owned, engineering and infrastructure construction management companies.

Through the World Biosphere Protection Treaty (WBPT), our critical forests and ocean ecosystems are recovering and are protected from future abuse. This unprecedented global treaty is a testament to our acceptance of responsibility for protecting our planet and our fellow humans. The world's governments, with substantial financial assistance from major energy conglomerates, banks, and pharmaceutical companies[3], have invested tens of trillions of dollars in this far-reaching treaty. WBPT has assisted hundreds of millions of people and their communities in preparing for the new realities of global warming, and it continues to manage and finance the restoration and ongoing preservation of the key components of Earth's biosphere.

I was born in 2018 and am about to turn 40, so I lived through the period I write about. I remember watching the first successful SSTO spaceplane flight in the late 2020s with my parents. WBPT was ratified when I was ten. I was seventeen when the first space elevator began operations. I made the trip to see the elevator (as have tens of millions of others), and it is a truly amazing feat of engineering. By the time I was in my thirties, I had been to space a few times. In 2052, I even met space's first birthed child, Alya, then eighteen, by chance at the Delta Spaceport. When I look back over these past thirty years, I am awed by the breadth and depth of humanity's ingenuity, focus, and accomplishments during this period — especially those of GEMI, IMPF, and WBPT.

During this tumulus period, GEMI, IMPF, and WBPT were at the forefront in the struggles to overcome some of our most daunting challenges. They worked to repair and protect Earth's biosphere, improve the human condition, and build the foundation for a space ecosystem. By 2053, GEMI leaders Drs. Baptista and Duarte had retired. Dr. Duarte, as a cultural anthropologist, had signed on for a multiple-year scientific expedition that began in late 2054. She is now in a mining colony on the edge of Jupiter's L4 trojan asteroid swarm studying evolving cultural shifts in long-term space communities. Dr. Baptista retreated to his New Mexico ranch, where he raises quarter horses and is a frequent judge at local rodeo events.

GEMI, with new leadership, remains a robust global organization dedicated to its original mission. IMPF, in contrast, finalized its dissolution in 2052, ending twenty-seven years of renovating and replacing the outdated and inefficient infrastructures of the world's largest cities — and making trillions of dollars for its investors. WBPT has matured into a vast international organization working closely with the IMF and the UN to monitor and administer the systems necessary — and occasionally enforce the treaty — to ensure the ongoing preservation of Earth's biosphere. Through their collective efforts, they helped build a healthier future here on Earth and in space, while cultivating cultural integrity and intellectual and economic equality for all.

----

[1]Regionalism has witnessed a revival around the world and is gaining traction in space, although the movement is still too new to predict how dominant it will become.

[2]The United Nations GEMS system recently predicted we will reach statistical net zero CO_2 emissions sometime late in 2057.

[3]WBPT member countries have essentially strong-armed corporations in numerous industries, through taxation and other means, into contributing nearly 50% of the yearly cost of WBPT programs worldwide.

About the Author

James Brown spent three years in the military (go Army!) and holds degrees in mathematics and business. He has worked on university scientific research teams, built businesses, and partnered with venture capitalists to meet shared goals. He is a lifelong technologist working within, and witnessing the evolution of, science and engineering disciplines around the world.

9 789898 957882 5